CHARLIE'S
REQUIEM

A GOING HOME NOVELLA

A. AMERICAN AND
WALT BROWNING

PROLOGUE

BY ANGERY AMERICAN

Going Home set a high bar for what life could look like after an EMP. But Morgan's journey and even his home focuses on more rural areas. The small towns of Florida are nothing compared to the chaos the tourist corridor would be like. Could you imagine being at Disney or Universal Studios when such an even occurred? What would those tens of thousands of people do? Where would they go?

If you've been following the series, you know the DHS isn't exactly concerned with the well being of the people of this country. But what are they really working towards? Who are they looking out for?

Morgan is doing his best to keep his small community safe, now let's take a look at Orlando and how Charlie deals with the crisis. It's a whole different situation surrounded by millions of residents and visitors all trying to survive.

I want to thank my good friend Walt Browning, who did a lot of the heavy lifting on this novella. Our teamwork has produced some fine work here. We hope you enjoy this and if you want more we will be happy to continue.

CHAPTER 1

Day 1

Orlando, FL

I hate the mornings. The boy thought. He silently dressed, trying to not be noticed. Mornings were some of the worse times of the day. Sometimes, if she stopped by the bar on the way home after working the late shift, the mornings could be painful. He hoped this was not one of those days. It was quiet in the house. That was usually a good sign.

The thin and wiry boy, almost a man at 17, meticulously folded his sleeping shorts and shirt, placing them in the upper right corner of his second of five drawers. The front of the shorts had to be pointing up and the shirt had to be folded like it had just been removed from its packaging. They always went into the same place. He only had the two sleeping shorts and shirts. The other pair, his favorites, were ready to be washed.

He would do the laundry when they left later that evening. His mom would be gone for dinner with her. They always went out to dinner. He always cooked for himself. He liked to cook for himself. He knew that the food was cleaned properly and that the plates and pans were sterile. He always cleaned the pots and pans before he cooked and did the same afterwards. The plates were stacked in neat and tidy rows in the cupboard and the utensils were aligned perfectly in their drawer. The kitchen was his place. They never cooked and as long as the beer and ginger ale for his mom's whiskey were in the front of the refrigerator, they left him and his little world alone. It was comforting to be able to control some of his environment when the rest of his existence was so disheveled and out of control.

He liked being in control when he could. Being around his mom and her girlfriend was never a good experience. Most of the time, he was ignored. Some of the time, he was noticed. Being noticed wasn't pleasant. The last time they noticed him, he still felt the pain from his swollen wrist and the cigarette burns. One of them got infected, but he knew how to handle that without involving anyone else. The antibacterial ointment usually took care of that. If it got worse, they had all kinds of medicine they had stolen from their jobs. Mom was a nurse at the hospital and her girlfriend was a nurse's aide at a retirement home. Most of the medicine they stole was to get high, but some of it was antibiotics. He knew how to use the antibiotics. He had learned of their uses many times. His mom and her girlfriend had seen to that over the years.

Mom and her girlfriend had been together for almost five years. His father got to see him every other weekend, but the judge wouldn't let him go over more than that. His father sold tools and supplies for a large hardware manufacturer and was not home during the week. He loved his weekends with his father and it made his mom and her girlfriend very angry. He never spoke about it until after last weekend. That's when they burned him again. He told them that he could leave the house when he turned 18 in a few months. They didn't like that at all. His wrist still hurt and was swollen. He told his teacher he hurt it playing football in the park by his house. She looked like she didn't believe him, but the cigarette burns were under his shirt and no one else knew about them. She sent him to the school nurse. It was his third visit in two months. She thought his wrist was broken, but he moved all his fingers and told the nurse he was going to the doctor that afternoon. She wrapped the wrist with an ACE bandage and let him go back to class.

The boy silently moved through his room, putting everything into its proper place. Assigning order to his life of chaos was one of the few things he did to keep his sanity. His clothing was pressed and all wrinkles were removed. His tennis shoes were spotless. He used his mom's white shoe polish when they got the occasional scuff-mark. His hair was always combed and off his ears. The guys thought he was weird. He ignored the girls. His mom had poisoned him on wanting to be with a girl.

He never understood his mother. Why she would hurt him was

unfathomable. Really, his mom rarely got involved, she just let her girlfriend hurt him. It had been five years since his mom and dad split up because his mom had met her, and the two had become a couple. That's when he and his mom left his dad and moved into her house.

His mom and her girlfriend shared not only a bed, but a growing problem with prescription pills. He wanted to tell his dad, but his mom's girlfriend said she would kill him if he ever told anyone. She was big and mean and looked like she meant what she had threatened. A few times she had beaten him so severely that he had to stay home from school. The past summer had been particularly difficult and the three months at home had nearly driven him mad. Twice he had ended up at his mom's hospital. Once with broken ribs and the other time with a concussion. Now, with school, at least he had time by himself. It was the mornings that brought so much fear. When the girlfriend drank and then got high, she was mean.

Finally, everything in his room was aligned and in its proper place, and the boy quietly left his room and walked towards the kitchen on his way out the door. His book bag was strapped over both shoulders, the weight evenly balanced so that it was both comfortable and perfectly aligned on his back.

Suddenly, he smelled the smoke. It wasn't the normal stale cigarette smoke that comes from a room that has had packs upon packs of cigarettes smoked in it over the years. It was the smell of fresh cigarette smoke, its acidity still strong with a sickening haze still floating in the air. The boy tentatively walked into the room, he had to pass through the kitchen to get out the outside door. That's when he saw her, sitting at the kitchen table, a nearly empty bottle of Jack Daniel's Tennessee Whiskey in front of the big, ugly woman that shared his mother's bed. She still had her dirty green scrubs on from the night shift. Her head slowly turned as the boy entered the room.

For his part, the boy moved as quickly and silently as he could, trying to get passed his captor. She was a large and lazy woman, really a man trapped in a woman's body. But before he could get away, she reached out and grabbed his injured right wrist and twisted it with all the force she could muster from her still sitting position. The force of the attack dropped the boy to his knees. But instead of pushing him to the ground like she always did, she stood up and still holding his hand, violently twisted his arm until he heard and felt a pop in his right shoulder. He screamed out in pain, kicking her in the knee. She dropped like a rock, hitting the floor with a heavy thud. The boy rushed back to his bedroom, his right arm hanging uselessly at his side, the joint dislocated from the socket. He stumbled into his room and slammed the door shut, locking the knob and staggering to the far wall.

Within seconds, the bedroom door exploded inward and the large, drunk woman shattered through the flimsy hollow core composite material and slammed into the boy, knocking him to the ground once again. She grabbed him by the neck and lifting him to his feet, she ran him into the jamb of the now shattered door.

"Now, now!" she hissed. "We can't have you going to school with a bad arm, now can we?"

She throttled the nape of his neck and grabbing the back of his pants by the belt, she slammed his dislocated shoulder into the corner of the door jamb, not once but three times, until the shoulder was popped back into place. She dragged him to the kitchen, depositing him on the floor. The boy laid dazed, his entire right side numb from the nerve damage of the assault.

The woman stormed to the kitchen table, looking for something. She returned with her pack of cigarettes and fumbling about, could find no lighter or matches. She cursed at him, and began tearing apart the kitchen while the boy lay on the floor, wishing that it was all just a terrible nightmare. His perfectly organized drawers were flung to the ground near his body, the forks and knives scattered on the floor he had just polished the night before to a waxy shine. Finally, the wretched woman found a pack of matches in one of the utility drawers. She ignited her cigarette and took a long drag on the stick. It glowed a sinister red as she reached down and tore back his shirt. With his right arm disabled, the boy could only scream as she plunged the burning cigarette over and over into his stomach. The boy began to lose all sense of time and space, his vision narrowing as the attack continued.

"So you want to leave your mother and me!" she screamed. "After all we have given your ungrateful ass. And you repay us by leaving!"

Another burning ember ignited pain on his right chest.

Suddenly, he heard his mother screaming nearby. **Oh God!** He thought. **Save me!**

"What have you done!" his mother screeched. "You ungrateful piece of crap! What have you done to make her so angry?"

His mother kicked him. Suddenly he felt his pants being ripped off. He cried out, but only received another kick in the side. The air left his lungs.

His left hand flailed on the floor, trying to find something to hold onto. Something to grab to pull himself up and get away. The forks scattered as his hand swung back and forth on the floor. Suddenly, an agonizing pain came from his groin, a burning flame seared through his body. He spasmed with a pain he had never, in his entire young life, experienced. His left hand found something and he swung it at the large woman, trying to get her off him. Trying to stop the pain.

The butcher knife arced toward his drunken attacker. She saw the six inch blade just a little too late. She tried to bring her arm up to stop the knife from striking her, but her alcohol laden brain was a little too numb to respond quickly enough. The blade rammed into her neck. She dropped to the ground, laying over the boy's legs, dead and bleeding on his fastidiously scoured floor.

His mother stood over them, her eyes dilated and fixed. She was in her scrubs as well, having fallen asleep after her night shift and having taken some of the OxyContin the two of them had stolen from their jobs. She screamed at the boy and launched herself onto his partially pinned body.

The boy snapped. His mother, the one person in the world that was there to protect and love her child, was trying to choke the life out of him. His mind, teetering on brink of breaking, shattered. His fixation on controlling his environment, his attempts to placate his mother and his docile acceptance of the abuse, all failed to stop the pain. His mind left him. His last sane thought was of the green scrubs that everyone in his life wore, at least everyone that had been hurting him. *Now,* his broken mind thought, *I will not be hurt anymore.*

He finally left the house over an hour later. He cleaned everything and put all back where it belonged. He scoured the floors and returned them back to the highly polished shine that they needed to have. He scrubbed the butcher knife and placed it into his backpack, just in case he needed to make himself safe once again. And when he finally shut the front door… when he left the house for the last time, he left no one behind alive. He was finally free.

CHAPTER 2

Charlie

Kirkman Specialty Clinic

Orlando, FL

Another scorcher, I thought. *The Florida heat can be such a bitch.*

I pulled into the medical center parking lot, looking for that rare shaded space. It was hard to find. Newer buildings like this one tended to have small trees and an immature landscape. Construction is always cheaper when you start with a blank slate, meaning a flat, empty piece of land. Finding some shade would be nice since it would keep the car's interior from getting baked while I visited. November normally brought temperate weather, but a weird warm front was touching Orlando as it cut across the southern half of the state. North of us, it was nice and cool, but we were going to have a few days of unusually hot weather.

Finding no shade, I reluctantly pulled into a space near the back of the lot. Thankfully, I was there on business and not as a patient. My company doesn't like phone calls from our clients complaining that their customer parking spaces were taken by my car. They don't want their patients inconvenienced by having to walk a few extra feet because the spaces toward the front are taken by non-patients like myself. I have no problem with that. I am fit and 28 years young. It's just humorous that the front three spots have a sign warning anyone not to park there. These spaces were reserved for the doctors. Just saying.

The Kirkman Specialty Clinic was just like most of the other clients on my route. A square piece of prefabricated concrete with a layer of sprayed-on stucco. Faux columns stood sentinel at the double-glass door entrance, giving the structure some modicum of class. It didn't work. It looked like all the other medical buildings I visit; Industrial cheap, gilded with cut-rate trappings. Inexpensive bronzed light fixtures oxidized in the Florida summer. Less than two years old, the hardware on the building was rusting and would have to be replaced, probably with more cheap hardware. A waste of money, if you ask me. But then again, no one said that doctors were good at anything other than their own profession. No one says that other than the doctors themselves. I have been on the job over six years and the stories I have heard of lost wealth were staggering. The doctors thought they were just as awesome in the stock market or land deals as they were in their own profession. Many found out they weren't. But that's a whole different story.

I popped the trunk on my Ford. I never would have bought a Ford, but I have to admit, the car is pretty sweet. Most of my friends were in a Toyota or some other Japanese or Korean car. Those models just had more "cool" when you're young. But this company car has taken good care of me these past two years. My upgrade would be coming soon; and I was going to be able to pick from three different models. I will probably get another Fusion.

I rolled my oversized sales briefcase behind me. It had all the new pamphlets and samples for our line of drugs. I hated that thing, just because it was so clunky looking. But given the amount of crap I have to bring with me, a large bag is a must.

"Hi, Charlie!" the receptionist sang.

"Hey Peg. How's it going?"

"Slammed as usual!" She replied with an expectant grin.

I handed over the loot. A large brown bag with handles from a local department store. The bag was only a disguise. You see, the Kirkman Specialty Clinic was a cardiology center, one of the finest in Central Florida. The loot was three dozen doughnuts. Not good for the patients to see three dozen doughnuts going into a heart center's break room.

Peg gave me a conspiratorial smile and took the bag to the back. I sat down in the reception area, glancing at the patients around me. The room wasn't too full, but I expected that. The only doctor here at this time was the senior partner. The other two were still at the hospital and wouldn't be back for another hour. It didn't matter though. Dr. Kramer was the senior partner; while the other two hadn't been out of their residencies for more than three years. He's a good man. Pushing 65, he has the reputation that the other two doctors use to enhance their status in the medical community. Their practice is a referral practice, and many of the patients often drive over an hour to see them. Dr. Kramer brings them in. He is the rainmaker. He likes me.

We share a common background since both of us graduated from the University of Florida. His undergraduate and medical degrees were from there, before his residencies at Duke University and Cleveland Clinic provided him with his specialty certification. I spent four years at Florida, getting my degree in chemistry while medaling on the school's swim team. We won several SEC championships while I was there. Dr. Kramer likes that. We both bleed orange and blue.

Dr. Kramer makes the buying decisions for the practice and has more influence on the other two doctors than I ever could. If you're in sales in the sunshine state, it helps if you are a Florida grad. And unlike most of the other salespeople in my profession, I have the scientific background to be intelligent about my products. It also helps that the drugs I sell really work. It makes my job much easier. And because Dr. Kramer likes me, I get good treatment from the staff. It also helps that I bring goodies for them; and doughnuts are always well received.

Peg came back to the desk and waved, holding up two fingers. Two minutes or twenty minutes to see the doctor. Only time will tell, so I smiled and waved back. I scanned the table beside me, bypassing many of the uninteresting magazines, finally finding one that I could read without wondering if the world would survive humanity. There is only so much celebrity gossip and mundane scandal you can read about before realizing that we worship people that don't deserve our time, let alone our entertainment money. I've been in the operating room, watching a cardiologist thread a microscopic camera into a man's ventricle and remove a life-threatening blood clot so that he could go home to his wife and children. I've watched emergency room staff restart dead hearts, breathe life back into drowned children and perform tasks that two generations ago would have been considered miracles. I never find them on the cover of the magazines. I guess if they got into a fight at a Las Vegas nightclub...

"Charlie! The doctor can see you now!" Peg said. So it was two minutes after all.

I rolled my cart behind me as I made my way back to his private office. Others in my profession have warned me about certain offices and some specific physicians having less than a professional approach to our relationship. In some offices, it can be a bit unnerving meeting with the doctor in his private room. One of the reasons I was hired was because of my age, as well as my background. And let's not kid around, you can get hired based on your looks. But I know Dr. Kramer and he is a good man and I've never gotten a bad vibe from him. Being fit and young, I can engender unwanted conversations. When you sell, you have to sell yourself as well as your product. Some doctors take that the wrong way. So I go by Charlie, which is short for Charlotte. Why Charlie? Hey, it's just too prissy.

CHAPTER 3

Day 1

Azalea Park Medical Clinic

Orlando, FL

The sunny day was pleasantly warm as Carol left the Urgent Care center. Lunch could not have come quick enough given the number of emergencies they had to handle this morning. With the flu season ramping up, the clinic had seen more than the typical number of runny nosed, body aching and lung hacking patients stumble in for treatment. All of these patients had failed to have the flu vaccine and most had waited too long to get to the clinic for the Tamiflu to be of optimal effect. Tamiflu is an anti-viral medication rather than a vaccine. For it to work on the flu virus, the patients needed to start taking the drug less than 48 hours from the onset of symptoms. Most of the patients had shown up after their symptoms had peaked three to five days into their infection, meaning the medication probably wouldn't help all that much.

She had 30 minutes to grab a bite to eat. She left her lab coat in the office, instead wearing her green scrubs without cover. It was warm enough on this November day to forego her white jacket, although HIPPA laws required that she was supposed to have a cover when leaving the office. She justified this oversight because she was going to use the drive through at a local fast food joint to get a drink and a salad, so she wouldn't be leaving her car.

She wandered over to the employee parking lot across the street from the clinic. She was fumbling with her phone, trying to get it out of her large and disorganized purse, when she noticed a young, thin man walking parallel to her. She stopped, pretending to search her purse for her keys, all the while keeping an eye on her unwanted guest. She noticed that he stopped as well. She continued to blunder about in her purse and assess her stalker, buying herself time to decide what to do.

He walked with a bit of a limp, his gate uneven. At first, she thought he had injured his leg. Then she realized that as he walked, his right side failed to swing and move normally. It was like his right arm was paralyzed. He began to circle around from where she had just come from, blocking her way back to the clinic. Her heart began to race as she realized the intent of this young and strange looking man. She quickly and smoothly removed a bottle of pepper spray from her purse and clicked it open. She continued toward her car, hastening her footsteps and quickly closing the distance between herself and the safety of her Honda.

Suddenly, she heard his footsteps racing toward her. She glanced back and saw that the young man had rapidly closed the distance between them. She would never make it to the car in time. She screamed and started running between the cars. His backpack kept catching on the edges of the automobiles as she ran amongst them. She heard his breath as he closed the gap between them. Terror filled her heart while the running took her breath, making it hard to scream. At one point, he grabbed her arm, only to have her break away as she sprinted between the rear bumper of a van and the front of an S.U.V. She heard him curse, and at one point, he mumbled loud enough to be heard.

"You'll never hurt me again!" he hissed.

What was he talking about? She thought. She didn't recognize him. *Maybe he was a disgruntled patient,* she found herself thinking as she dodged back toward the clinic.

As she sprinted back across the street, he grabbed her with his left hand. She spun around and bringing up the pepper spray, she hosed his face with the caustic liquid.

The young man cried out, letting go of her with his good hand, he covered his face and crashed to the street. Carol ran back into the office, crying out for help. A minute or two passed before she was calm enough to relate her story. When the doctor and a male nurse finally made it outside, the young man was gone.

They called the police and a couple of patrol cars arrived within minutes. After taking her statement, the two officers called in the description of the suspect. A white male, short cropped brown hair with a noticeable limp or paralysis of the right side. Jeans, polo shirt and a backpack last seen near the intersection of Colonial Drive and Bumby Avenue. The police assured the young woman that it was likely an attempted purse snatcher or carjacker, but with no weapon noted, the report would only suggest assault with possible strong armed theft. Given his rambling murmurs, it was likely that the young man was looking for quick money to feed his drug habit. She was told not to worry anymore about it and that she had done well to protect herself. The clinic let her go home, but she did stop on the way to replace the used can of pepper spray.

~ * * * ~

Orlando police officer John Drosky had been on the force for nearly eight years. In all that time, he had never had to draw down on a suspect. He found that most situations required a calm voice and open heart. The few times he had deployed his weapon were as backup to an already violent situation. In all three of those situations, the suspects had surrendered to one of the other police officers on the scene.

The call announcing the assault at the Urgent Care clinic came over his radio. The incident had occurred only a half a mile away, and Drosky replied to dispatch that he had received the A.P.B. The young officer turned at the next cross-street and reversed back toward the intersection of Colonial and Bumby, his head on a swivel as he searched for anyone matching the description given by the victim.

The officer had traversed about a quarter of a mile back, driving on a street one block south of Colonial Drive, when he saw a young man walking with a strange gait down the sidewalk. One look at his face, red and flush from tears and a possible dousing by pepper spray, told the policeman all he needed to call in a possible suspect sighting from the clinic attack.

Drosky stopped the vehicle and turned on his blue strobe lights. He exited the vehicle and rocked the hood forward on his Safariland SLS holster, freeing his Sig 226 for a quick draw. He slowly approached the young man, noting the lack of movement of his right arm. The physical description couldn't have been more accurate. The backpack, jeans and polo shirt were a perfect match in color. The young man moved as in a daze, mumbling under his breath as he slowly wandered down the sidewalk. He moved without a purpose, his mind unfocused even though Drosky's police car stood just a few yards away with its lights flashing.

"Sir!" the office said. "Stop right there and keep your hands where I can see them!"

The officer had his right hand on his service pistol, ready to draw it if any sign of violence were to occur. The policeman pointed with his left hand at the boy.

"Sir!" he repeated. "Stop and keep your hands where I can see them."

The young man, really a teenager, suddenly looked up and noticed the officer. He gave the policeman a funny look, like he had just woken up, and did the craziest of things. He smiled.

"Sir! Please do me a favor and stop. Keep your hands away from your body."

The teenager stopped and turned to the officer, his hands away from his body, palms open and facing out.

"Young man," the officer said in a more quiet tone, "please lay face down on the sidewalk."

The teenager responded as ordered. He unsnapped his backpack, letting it drop to the ground. The young man went prone, and officer Drosky came up behind him and helped him spread his legs and arms, almost like a snow angel.

"Son," the officer said. "Do you have any weapons? Any drugs or needles I need to know about?"

The boy pointed at his backpack, but said nothing. After carefully patting him down, the officer placed the boy in handcuffs. Another patrol car rolled up allowing Drosky a chance to search his backpack. The officer was surprised to see high school books and notepads, all neatly packed and perfectly maintained. After removing all of the school items, he opened the flap on the side of the bag. He shook his head and reaching in with gloved hand, gently removed a kitchen butcher knife.

"I have a weapon," Drosky announced.

A shame, the officer thought. If the stupid kid hadn't had the knife, he could have been out on the street tonight. Even though he hadn't brandished it to the victim, it wouldn't sit well that it was in his possession.

"What is your name?" Drosky asked.

No reply. Both officers tried to get the young man to talk. He refused to say a word. Instead of being afraid, or belligerent or acting like most other young drug addicted youths did, the boy just lay there with a slight smile on his face. Drosky had never seen a perp look so sedate, so content with his lot in life. Most druggies talked. They denied or pleaded with him. This one just didn't. No words. No violent or angry attitude. Nothing about this guy indicated he was capable of assaulting another human being.

Drosky radioed in that the suspect was in custody and ready for him to transport. He had his wallet and learned that although he was still 17, the presence of a large knife linked to a violent attack mandated that they take him to the 33rd street jail for processing with the criminal adults.

Drosky just shrugged. It wouldn't be pleasant for this young man, being thrown into prison with adults that would love to see such a pretty young man come into their midst. Hopefully, the judges would see that. He had no criminal record that they could pull up when he called in his name and address. *Such a waste,* Drosky thought.

They put the young man into the back of Officer Drosky's patrol car. He sat without complaint, even though his right side appeared to be non-functional.

"I'm taking you to the 33rd street jail," the officer said. "When you get there, let them know who to call so you can get some help."

The boy/man just sat in the back seat, the simple smile still plastered on his face.

"Son," the officer said. "Look at me, please."

The boy turned and looked at the policeman.

"Who are you going to call? Do you have anyone you can contact?"

The boy stared at him, and finally gave his head a slight shake.

"Jesus, can't you say anything? Talk to me!"

The boy murmured something and smiled at the kind policeman.

"What did you say? Can I help you in any way?"

"No," the boy finally said with a sedate grin on his face.

"Good lord, son. Why in the hell are you smiling like that? Don't you know where you're going?"

The boy nodded.

"Then why in God's green earth are you smiling?"

"I'm free," he whispered. The boy turned his head and faced forward. Officer Drosky made a note in his report to consider a psyche evaluation. The kid wasn't right, and he needed help. As they drove down to the jail, Drosky could only hope his report would push the kid in the right direction. With nearly 4000 inmates or suspects at the jail, he knew deep in his heart that the kid would probably be lost in the system. *Damn it,* he thought.

The minutes passed silently as they made their way to the jail. No other words were uttered as the sally port opened and the officer drove into the holding area where the suspects were removed from his car and processed into the legal system. The sally port, a secure, controlled entry into the jail, reminded Drosky of the gates in Jurassic Park. It was a reality check for the prisoners that they were entering a dangerous and unpredictable place. Most of the arrested would comment on the doors the first time they saw them. His prisoner said no words.

As the doors closed behind him, Drosky looked at the kid in his rear view mirror. *This kid isn't going to last one week in there,* he thought. *Well, nothing I can do now. He made his own bed, now he'll have to sleep in it.* At least, that's what Officer Drosky told himself as he led the young man into the bowels of the jail. Telling himself that was the only way he could sleep at night.

Processing the young man was remarkably smooth. The only thing that put a wrench into the whole procedure was the boy's lack of desire to contact anyone. He answered every question and cooperated in every way other than providing a next-of-kin phone number. The staff at the jail tried to look up the boy's last name in the directory, but no phone number came up. He didn't tell them that he had been living with his mother who only had a mobile phone and no land line. Not that it would have helped to have a land line. His mother had kept her maiden name and the boy had his father's last name.

The young man smiled when he thought how he had told his mom that he was keeping his dad's last name. She had pressed him to change his last name to hers when he turned 18, hoping to provide her with yet another knife to stab his father with. When he denied her this, she looked like she was going to explode. The girlfriend let him know later that day how much she disapproved of his disrespect for his mother. That wasn't a pleasant night. But he didn't have to worry about that anymore. No one would hurt him again! His grin became a bit wider at the thought.

"We need to send a patrol car over to his address," the booking officer told Drosky. "He's not 18 yet and his parents need to be notified."

"I can do it," he replied. "My shift ends at five, and I can make it my last stop."

"Here's my number," the officer said. "Call me when you make contact and give them this." She handed the officer a business card with the BRC (Booking and Releasing Center) phone number on it.

"I don't know if he's going to be processed as an adult or child," she continued. "It's late, but I'll be setting up an initial hearing with the judge this afternoon or early evening. I'd like to know where he will be processed, either here or at juvie."

"I should know by five or so," the officer replied. "I'll call you directly when I meet with his parents."

"Thanks John," she replied. "I appreciate you looking into this."

"Atta girl!" came a snide remark from one of the other processing clerks. "Saint Beth to the rescue! I mean, come on. Just process the stupid shits and quit trying to save the world. They're all a bunch of perverts and assholes!"

Beth just shook her head and shrugged her shoulders.

"No problem, Beth. I'll touch base with you as soon as I see what's going on." John finally replied as he stood and left the office.

The young man was processed. Fingerprints and pictures were taken and the digital images were placed into the county's database. He was led to a large holding cell where he joined several other suspects that had been arrested earlier that day. The young boy looked about and saw a few other souls milling about or sitting in the spacious room. No one paid any attention to him other that a quick first glance to size him up. He presented them with no threat, and they all looked away once again. He quietly sat down on a padded bench and leaned back against the wall and thought about what he had done that morning. His father would be relieved that he didn't have to deal with his ex-wife anymore. Closing his eyes, he quickly fell fast asleep, getting his first good rest since he was at his father's house two weekends ago. *Finally*, he thought, *life was good.*

CHAPTER 4

Day 1

Charlie

Kirkman Specialty Clinic

"Charlie, how are you doing?" he said. He reached out and gave me a warm and firm handshake.

"Really well, thanks." I genuinely replied.

"Can you believe that darned football team?" he started.

The good doctor loved to talk football. Every Florida grad does. They breathe the game; and it is football season. That means a lot of football conversation. I had never been a big football fan; at least I hadn't until I went to college in the SEC. Football is its own religion in the south. You either love SEC football, or you don't open your mouth. It's November, and Florida was having a tough year. They won the games they should have won, but seemed to find ways to lose games they had a chance of winning. It was frustrating, given the recent success they had under their last head coach when they had won two national championships during his tenure. Now they just tried to remain relevant in the tough SEC eastern division. At least they weren't in the western division where at least three or four of the teams had a serious chance at the national title. Because of this, I found that reading the local Orlando sports page was as much a part of my job as the research summaries the company had us learn. I read both with a passion, even reading the entire research papers rather than just the summaries so I could speak frankly with my clients.

"So Charlie," he started. "I've read a bit about your company's new drug. The results are promising."

I knew he was testing me. He did that to everyone around him. It's what makes him great at his profession, and what I personally loved about him. He didn't tolerate bullshit. When other reps came in and touted their drug, he usually saw through the flaws and called them on it. My drugs worked and were relatively inexpensive. He cared about both of those things. That's how he built his reputation. He cares.

"To date, and with the limited size of the sample group, I'd say we are on the right track!" I replied.

Our new drug, Cardaxapro, was a cardiac medication that had the added benefit of decreasing the uptake of Calcium in the cardiac muscle. In other words, it increased the blood flow to the heart muscle while it effectively controlled blood pressure as a side effect. Two or three medications were taken care of by our one pill.

"I would caution you that the sample size of the experimental group was not as large as I would have liked," I added.

"I agree," he said with a smile. I scored a point or two with him, recognizing that drug companies often cherry picked their results to put a good spin on their product. I read the study and saw the limited size of the group.

"Don't worry about it," he said. "The study was done at John's Hopkins. The cardiology team there doesn't have an agenda. Besides, 340 patients tested is enough."

"What I liked is that their data collection was over a five-year period." I added.

Dr. Kramer smiled. He took the pamphlet but never bothered to read it. He knew it was full of a lot of fluff and pretty pictures. The real meat of the studies he had reviewed in his professional journals like *Cardiology* and *The New England Journal of Medicine*. He knew that the drug would work.

I was about to bring up some of the side effect when the lights briefly flickered and the office went quiet. Everything shut down. The lights, the computers and the air conditioner just stopped working.

"Crap," I blurted. "Another brown out?"

Dr. Kramer went to his office door and called down the hall.

"Peg," he shouted. "Hit the backup generator and call the power company!"

A few moments later, the power returned and everything came back to life. I felt the breeze of the air conditioner on my face. Life was good again.

We began to discuss the drug when we were interrupted by Peg. She knocked on the door and entered immediately.

"Dr. Kramer, we have a problem."

"What is it?" he asked. "It seems that the generator is working, but we don't actually have any procedures in place now, do we?"

The practice had installed backup generators for just such an occasion. They routinely ran stress tests in the back rooms which required constant monitoring of the patient's vital signs while they ran on a treadmill. Occasionally, they did a Thallium stress test that chemically stimulated the heart. These patients had a much more fragile profile and couldn't walk a treadmill without a significant risk of an acute outcome. In other words, they could die if they exercised too much.

"No, doctor." Peg replied. "It's just that none of the phones work."

"That's strange," he replied. "Then you can use my cell phone."

"That's what I mean," she said with some concern. "The cell phones don't work either. I mean they don't work at all. They won't even power up."

"All of them?" he incredulously asked.

"None of ours at the front desk. And two patients said their phones are dead too."

Dr. Kramer opened his desk drawer and took out his iPhone. He hit the power button but nothing happened. He grabbed a charger cord and plugged it into the wall outlet. After a minute, he tried to power the device up again while still attached to the wall outlet. Again nothing.

I pulled out my iPhone and I had the same problem. It was dead.

"What the hell," he said.

I was in shock. I have never heard him say anything derogatory or mean about anything or anybody. Swearing was so out of the ordinary for him, I became concerned. So did Peg. She got a very bad look on her face.

Just then, a nurse came to the now open office door and peered in.

"Doctor Kramer," she started. "I think something's wrong outside."

"What's going on now, Janice?" he cautiously asked.

"My car died," she replied.

"It won't start?"

"No," she said. "I mean it just died as I was driving out of the parking lot. Everything just went dead. It won't even begin to crank when I push the start button. It's like someone just took out the battery."

"Where is it now?"

"Still sitting in the parking lot."

The three of us followed Janice out the front door. The backup generator was making quite the racket, but the din slowly dissipated as we left the front entrance. Janice's car was at the far end of the parking lot, sitting in the exit lane.

I ran to my car and pushed the fob. Nothing. I hit button a second and third time; still nothing. I extracted the emergency key that was imbedded inside the fob and manually opened the door to the car and got in. I pushed the start button on the dashboard and was met with perfect silence. The car was dead, totally dead. I got out and looked over at Janice's vehicle. The three of them just stood next to the dead automobile and stared out onto Kirkman road. The office sat on a six lane thoroughfare about a mile from Universal Studios. At this time of day, traffic was usually heavy. I followed their gaze and looked out of the parking lot and onto the busy street. Nothing was moving. Cars were pulled to the side of the road or sat dead in the middle of the heavily travelled street. People were out of their cars, holding their cell phones to their ears and trying to work the buttons. Frustration was already beginning to build as they were all having problems with their technology. Dead cars and dead phones make a bad combination. Several men were pushing a number of cars to the side of the road, while others just stood in the street, looking for someone to come and help.

Dr. Kramer slowly walked back to me and gently grabbed my arm. The four of us walked back into the building and went directly to the break room.

"Dismiss the patients but let them know that their cars aren't working," he said to Peg. "Then I want all the staff and patients to gather in the reception area in five minutes."

Peg and Janice split up to deliver his message; Peg to the front and Janice to the rear treatment areas.

"Come with me," he gently said. I followed him into his office and he shut the door.

He tried to boot his computer but had no luck, so he turned to me in his chair. I sat across from him not knowing what was happening or what he was about to say.

"Charlie," he started. "Where do you live?"

"Orlando," I replied, unsure where this was going.

"No, where in Orlando?"

"Baldwin Park," I replied. Baldwin Park is a planned community that sprang up about 20 years ago when the Navy closed down a large base on the east side of town. The large lake and newly available property were scooped up by a city-approved development group. A colonial style 1100-acre miniature city was created with a planned mixture of trendy condominiums and traditional New England style homes, all packed into the former federally-owned land.

"That's not too bad," he said. "You're only about 10 to 15 miles away."

"I suppose so; I've never measured it. I just plan my day around traffic. It's about 25 minutes from here with normal traffic."

"That means nothing now," he cryptically replied. "Nothing's normal now."

"What do you mean?" I tentatively asked.

Peg entered the private office and informed the doctor that everyone was in the waiting room.

"Just follow me," he said. We moved down the hall into the reception room. Almost 20 people stared at us when we entered the common area.

"Please, sit down." Dr. Kramer requested. Everyone did as they were told.

"We have a total power outage outside. We've lost more than the electricity," he continued. "All land lines and cell phones are out of order as well. In fact, everything electronic seems to be down."

"What happened?" One of the patients asked.

"I don't know," he honestly replied. "But things don't look good. All the cars outside on the road are dead as well. Everyone is stranded."

"But we have lights here," the patient stated.

"We have a generator," he replied.

"Why is it working and nothing else does?" someone else asked.

"I truly don't know," he said. "We had it installed with a lightning protective screen around it. Maybe that kept it from going out. All I know is that nothing outside this building seems to be on."

Panicked conversations began as the assembled group tried to deal with their new reality. Dr. Kramer hushed them. Talking loudly, he finally silenced the group and continued speaking.

"We don't know how extensive this is," he continued. "It may just be our area; or it may be larger than that. I would recommend that you stay here until we figure this out. At least with our generator, we will have power for the next few days."

"FEW DAYS?" Another patient gasped. "What do you mean a few days?"

"Just what I said," he replied. "We don't know how long this will last. If it's local, I would expect emergency services to be here shortly. If it is more widespread, we could be looking at an extended period of time."

"Just how extended?" Another patient asked.

"No way to know," he said. "But let's just take this one step at a time."

Dr. Kramer organized the group. He got a list of medications his patients were taking and had us all check the medicine locker for replacements. I volunteered my stash and he gratefully accepted. The patients were given water and shown where the bathroom facilities were. The cable was out, so the staff tried to put on some old movies over the DVD connection but neither the television nor the DVD player would work. They all sat in silence as Dr. Kramer went back to his office, and I followed along.

After he shut the door, he sat heavily in his chair and looked at me. I sat down without prompting and faced him. He looked both tired and worried and I quickly realized that I had never seen him like this before. Here was a man that literally held people's lives in his hands and he was afraid. After seeing his demeanor, I became afraid too.

"So what's really happening?" I asked.

"I think we were hit by an EMP," he replied.

"An EMP? What's that?"

"Electromagnetic Pulse. A burst of electromagnetic energy that overwhelms electronic equipment. It basically fries anything that uses electricity."

"How? What could cause this?"

"Well," he continued, "A lot of things can cause an EMP. Nature creates them with a lightning strike, but given the large area that's affected, I doubt that is the cause. Solar flares can cause this as well. We could have been hit by a solar EMP."

"How many are affected then?"

"It could be just us, or all of the east coast. He replied. It could affect the entire nation; or it could be global. But that's only if the cause was solar."

"What else could have caused it then?"

"A nuclear detonation would do that," he somberly replied.

"WHAT?"

"I didn't see any mushroom clouds when we were outside," he said with some conviction. "If there was a nuclear detonation and it caused this outage, it would have most likely been about 200 miles up in the air, and would hardly be noticed here on the ground. At least the blast wouldn't be noticed, but the damage we see around us could be from just such an event."

I was stunned. Either scenario sounded bleak. A thousand things ran through my mind. *My family*, I thought. *What about my family?*

My parents were divorced almost two decades ago. My mother brought another man into our house after asking my dad to leave. In the long run, it was probably for the best. My dad remarried five years later and lived nearby, but was up in North Carolina for a few weeks. My mom moved to Tampa to be with yet another guy. She was always looking for something better, playing the victim whenever things didn't work out. I forgave her, but promised myself I would never be like her. So far, I was doing OK. But with my family far away, I had nowhere to go other than my apartment. I lived alone.

"I could use your help," Dr. Kramer said, breaking me out of my trance. "If you can, I need you to help me with what's coming in the next few days."

"I guess so," I replied. "I don't have any family in town anyway. What do you need me to do?"

He laid out a plan that seemed excessive, but I had learned to trust him over the past six years. He had never lied to me or let me down. I did what he asked.

CHAPTER 5

Day 1

Officer John Drosky

On Patrol, Orlando, FL

Officer John Drosky keyed his radio and reported back to dispatch that he was going "10-6" or "Busy-Unless Urgent" to stop by the boy's house on his way "back to the barn" at the end of his shift.

The boy lived just a few miles from where he had been arrested, and Drosky found the house with little trouble. The one story concrete block home sat in an older district of the city. The neighborhood was a combination of trendy and tired. Several homes had replaced their older jalousie windows with more modern double hung replacements. These homes showed signs of being well maintained, their lawns manicured and plant beds lined with plastic or wood edgers. Most of the open car ports were empty. It was mid-afternoon and the homeowners were still at work. The officer was pleasantly surprised that both car port spots were occupied when he found the young man's home. But as he suspected, the home showed no sign of improvement or maintenance that would indicate a stable family life. It always seemed to be this way.

John stopped his car in front of the house, staying out of the driveway. He walked up the broken asphalt and down the weed infested concrete front walkway. He rang the doorbell and waited. After a minute, he rang it once again and followed it with several loud and resounding raps on the door.

After another minute passed, he cautiously strolled around the side of the house, shaking his head at the weeds and detritus that covered the overgrown yard. He cautiously approached the back door and knocked loudly, announcing himself.

"HELLO!" he yelled. "Orlando police. Please open the door!"

No response. The officer looked into the window and saw what appeared to be a living room and across from him, the front door. No lights were on. He retraced his steps and pressing his face to the next window, he stared in to the kitchen. It was remarkably clean and organized. *Surprising!* He thought. He moved towards that back of the house where he had first walked around from the front and, shielding his eyes, he pressed his face once again against the pane of glass and stared into the back room.

It looked like a large bedroom. The mini-blinds were partially closed, limiting the light entering the room as well as his ability to see directly in. He pulled out his Surefire flashlight and held it against the glass, providing some light to see by. He looked once again into the room and saw two people under the cover, sleeping in the king-sized bed.

Damn it, he thought. *They're either assholes or drugged out.*

He knocked heavily on the window, yelling through the glass.

"ORLANDO POLICE!" he shouted. "OPEN THE DOOR NOW!"

No one moved inside the bed. Not a peep, not even a shrug or turn.

Officer Drosky got a sinking feeling in his gut. He knew what he was looking at, but his mind didn't want to believe it. He had to force himself to return to the back door. He didn't want to confirm his deepest fears. He tried the doorknob and found it open. He pulled out his Sig 226 and using his flashlight, he entered the house, announcing his presence.

"THIS IS THE ORLANDO POLICE," he shouted. "IS THERE ANYONE HOME?"

The tired home refused to reply. Drosky cautiously cleared the large room and made his way back to the bedroom where the two bodies laid. By now, he knew they were bodies. He slowly made his way back to the bedroom and found two women under the sheets. Both wore hospital scrubs and their final embrace was marred by an open stab wound to the neck on one of the women, and a stab wound to the chest on the other. Their eyes had been closed and the smaller woman's head lay on the other's shoulder. Drosky thought of the kitchen knife the young man had in his backpack. The blade of that knife matched the death blows that stared back at him. He shook his head in sorrow. He hated to make the call to Beth. The kid was going in with the adults and with the death penalty alive and well in the state of Florida, Officer John Drosky knew the kid wasn't in for a very happy future.

John tried his portable radio, but was only rewarded with a busy beep, so he walked back to his cruiser and stared back at the house.

Goddamn it, he thought. *Why couldn't things just come out right for a change?* He sat down in his cruiser and turned on the engine. It was remarkably warm for November and the air conditioner would feel nice after getting out of the stuffy, tired old home.

Just as John grabbed the mic to his encrypted Motorola APCO 25 Digital Radio System, his car died. It just stopped working. He tried to crank the engine but got no response. His car had turned into a dead lump of metal. Nothing came on. It was as if someone had pulled out his car's battery.

John shook his head, thinking that this was just one of those days. He grabbed his mobile phone and was just as surprised when he saw that it had no power either. He got out of his car, staring at the iPhone, jabbing at the power button on top of the phone. Nothing.

And that's when he noticed it. The sound of nothing. The boy's neighborhood was only a block from a major road. Traffic noise was heavy with commuters filling the four lane road on their journey home. Now, the noise was gone, replaced by birds and a faint sound an occasional yell or scream coming from the normally congested streets.

John ran up to the intersection and stared down the normally busy thoroughfare. Everywhere, cars were stopped. People were out of their vehicles, yelling at each other both in confusion and a bit of fear as they searched for an answer that made sense to them. Several cars had collided as they lost power, their drivers frantically trying to call 911 or whomever their closest loved-one was.

John instantly knew what had happened, or at least what likely had happened. Since 2010, the city had been integrating their terror units with the federal government. All of the officers had received training on CBRN (Chemical, Biologic, Radiologic and Nuclear) emergency situations. The

OPD had been actively coordinating their efforts with FEMA's Center for Domestic Preparedness (CDP) out of Alabama. Due to the city's large tourist population, Orlando was considered a high priority target. Because of this training, John recognized all the symptoms of an EMP event. His initial exposure to this training inspired him to further his education on the subject. Because of this, he was pretty sure this attack was a big one. Not a car moved for as far as he could see.

Suddenly, he heard a scream and saw several people pointing to the sky. John couldn't help but watch as a large commuter plane was slowly gliding over Colonial drive when it suddenly started to fall from the sky, spinning down from the heavens, it exploded not a mile away from him. Just as quickly, he could see almost a dozen more aircraft, some filled with hundreds of souls, rapidly descending from the clouds. *If this was nation-wide*, he thought, *tens-of-thousands of people were dying right now!*

It was too much for him to take, and he sat down on the sidewalk and silently watched. Armageddon had arrived and John knew that the city of nearly two million had no clue what had just happened. Seeing the metal tubes, tombs really, dropping rapidly from the sky reinforced his belief that there was little chance that these people would survive the next few weeks.

CHAPTER 6

Day 1

Delta Flight 2181

3000 feet over Orlando

Captain Kevin Stillwagon concentrated on his instruments as Delta flight 2181 was making its final north to south approach to Orlando International Airport. The cabin was silent as the captain and his first officer observed sterile cockpit protocol which mandated no conversation save necessary observations or recommendations which identified less than nominal events or environmental changes. In other words, the two pilots shut up unless something seemed out of sorts.

The approach into Orlando from their present northern flight pattern was one of Captain Stillwagon's least favorite. Their approach brought them near the Orlando Executive Airport, which was less than 10 miles north of OIA. This meant that their approach to Orlando International had to be modified to not interfere with local civilian aviation traffic. This modified landing vector required that he maintain an altitude of 2500 feet until he passed the Executive airport, then a rapid descent to the sweet spot of 1000 feet during his final approach.

Originally, Orlando Executive was the civilian aviation hub of the city until the early 1960's when civilian jetliners began to ply the skies over central Florida. Landlocked by the growing city, the tiny airport's runways were insufficient to handle the new jet's needs. Fortunately, just 10 miles south, the Air Force had a large and capable airfield and the federal government partnered with the city of Orlando to create a joint military-civilian airport using facility's military designation, McCoy Airfield. For the next 12 years or so, Boeing 707 civilian jets shared runway time with B-52 Statofortresses and KC-135 Stratotankers. Both civilian and military jets played a critical role in the defeat of Communism. The military jets flew 24 hour, 7 day a week missions for NORAD as the military doctrine of MAD (mutually assured destruction) required that nuclear weapons be deployed and available at a moment's notice as a deterrent to a surprise military strike. The civilian side allowed for the necessary economic growth in central Florida that led to Disney World and other money-making endeavors. This created a bigger tax base that could support the massive military costs needed to keep the B-52 bombers or "BUFFs" in the air. The inferior economics of Communism couldn't keep up with the economic might of a free society and it eventually bankrupted the Soviet Union, ending the cold war.

In 1976, the last military flight had departed McCoy Airfield. The city and state renamed it Orlando International Airport, but to this day, the airport designation you see on your check-in bags has the old airfield three-letter abbreviation, MCO.

Now, about 10 miles out, Captain Stillwagon was fighting a stiff crosswind that cut southwest to northeast across his nose. A steady 25-knot wind was forcing him to use his considerable skills in keeping the nose of the jet on a steady trajectory. Having been a commercial pilot for over 20 years, the situation was far from dire, but required some skill to keep his passengers comfortable. His Airbus 320's twin engines were powering them through the sunny skies. Were it not for the crosswind and his modified flight trajectory, the next few minutes would be a breeze.

His first officer, Tyler Landrey, was sitting in the next seat reviewing the approach checklist and monitoring their instrument readings. At 3000 feet and about 9 miles now from the airport, they were getting ready for the final and quick descent to the runway. To their right, Stillwagon could see Highway 50 cutting an east/west line through the city. The executive airport could be seen as well, just a few miles east sitting just south of the highway. In a few more seconds, they would begin to initiate their landing checklist: landing gear down, flaps at full and reduced power to the engines. At 2500 feet, their "Gip Wiz" or ground proximity warning system, would start counting down the feet above ground. In a normal landing, the mechanical voice would be the only "conversation" heard in the cockpit as they made their final descent.

All commercial flights are to make, what are called, powered landings. This means that no commercial airline would shut down the engines until 100 feet or less above the runway. When these engines are shut down, the restart time can exceed 15 seconds. If an obstacle were to suddenly appear on the runway such as a wayward luggage cart or vehicle, a powered landing would allow the pilot to instantly accelerate and keep the airliner in the air for another landing pass.

With over 30,000 pounds of thrust from each of its two engines, the A320 sliced its way toward OIA when the unthinkable happened. The entire jetliner lost power. Instantly, flight 2181 went from a modern, sleek passenger airline to an aluminum tube hurtling through the air with about 90 seconds of glide time before gravity brought it to the ground.

"FUCK!" Landrey shouted. "Engines off line, all power gone!"

"No shit!" Stillwagon shot back.

The entire control panel in front of the two men went dark. The modern jet was both blessed and cursed with fly-by-wire controls, which means that almost everything is computer controlled. Older planes and early jets used wires to control the aircraft's yoke (pitch and roll) as well as the left/right or "yaw" movement of the plane. In older craft, the cables literally pulled on the flaps to create the proper movement. Now, computers sent an electronic signal that powered the flaps. With the power off, nothing happened. Everything was frozen in the last position that the computer had directed it to.

"Take the controls!" Stillwagon said to his first officer.

As commander of the aircraft, he was responsible for the lives of the souls sitting behind him. His first priority was to restart the engines which meant that he had to pass the control of the aircraft, what little they had, over to his co-pilot.

Within seconds, Kevin determined that he had no engine control and wouldn't within the next minute or two, when gravity dictated that they would be on the ground. Their only hope was finding somewhere to set down, without power and with little control of the situation.

"We can make it to the field!" Landrey loudly said. "We've still got rudder and the trim wheel!"

All modern (post mid 1980's) commercial aircraft are equipped with an emergency system known as the "RAT" or ram air turbine. When power is lost to the aircraft, a gravity latch releases and a turbine drops from the airframe. The 200 mile per hour wind rushing through the turbine spins its blades powering a small generator or APU (auxiliary power unit) to maintain hydraulic pressure and provide some flight control.

The pilots now had two controls available to direct their aircraft. The rudders to control their yaw, or left/right direction, and the one cable controlled instrument on the aircraft, their trim tab. The trim tab is a small tab or mini-flap which is part of the rear elevator. It gave them some elevator control or the nose up and nose down pitch of the plane.

"We have the airspeed to get to OIA!" Landrey said. "The hydraulics are responding but sluggish."

"That's the RAT kicking in," Stillwagon replied. "Our airspeed is down to 190 and we are approaching 2500 feet."

The only three controls that were still functional without electricity were the air speed, the altimeter and the attitude or "horizon". Kevin could see his speed, how high he was and if the wings were level with the ground. That was it.

"We can't risk the airport," Stillwagon stated. "It's pushing our glide path limits. That crosswind won't let us stay on track either! It's at least 25 knots. We don't have the rudder control to compensate. We'll drift left into wherever the crosswind pushes us!"

"Then what the fuck do you want to do?" Landrey replied.

The captain scanned the landscape in front of him. They were following a major roadway directly under their wings. The six lane road ran directly to the airport, but at rush hour, the roadway was full of cars and trucks. A quick look down showed a full thoroughfare, and as he continued to scan for some field or body of water to touch down onto, he could swear that the cars were all stopped on the street. Even the ones that weren't at a traffic light.

No time for that now. Off to the southwest, Kevin noted two large bodies of water that would handle an emergency landing. He did a lot of quick math in his head and determined that Lake Conway was likely their best bet to set the aircraft down without creating any additional damage or deaths. First and foremost, Kevin was responsible for the over 150 souls on his plane. But he couldn't risk killing more innocents if putting his plane down had little chance of saving his passengers while hurting others on the ground. If no legitimate option became available, Captain Stillwagon would find a field or spot where he would do the least damage and point his nose into the ground, minimizing collateral damage. It was a horrible situation to be in.

"Over there," Kevin pointed to his counterpart. "Aim of those two bodies of water. It's into the crosswind and within five miles."

"You sure about this?" Landrey said back. Fear could be heard in his voice and Kevin couldn't blame him for it. He was about to piss his own pants, but as captain, he couldn't have the option of showing any hesitation or dread.

"Yeah," Kevin replied. "I'll take us in. Just line me up while I inform the passengers and crew."

Kevin picked up a telephone that was directly wired into the passenger cabin. It wasn't connected to any computers or other switches. He keyed the microphone and spoke to the souls riding behind him.

"This is the captain speaking!" the speakers blared to the horrified tourists.

When the lights went out in the plane, even the most white-knuckled travelers accepted the first few seconds. But when several people noticed that the engine noise had stopped, pandemonium erupted. It had been less than 30 seconds since the plane died, and terror had already set in.

"We have lost all power to the aircraft," he continued. "This is a red emergency. We have 60 seconds to get ready. Flight attendants, prepare for ditching!"

Kevin had informed the flight attendants that there was a "red" emergency. It was one of three emergency landings that he could have announced. The first was a medical emergency, which is self-explanatory. The second is a "yellow" emergency, which indicated the aircraft was somewhat disabled but that no injuries or damage was expected. The third emergency was a "red" emergency. That meant all bets were off and to expect damage to the aircraft and possible injury or death. The fact that he informed them that he was "ditching" meant a water landing. Finally, he told them to expect this all to happen in about 60 seconds.

The attendants unstrapped themselves from their jump seats and rushed down the aisles commanding everyone to stay seated and get into a crash position. Children started crying and screaming, their theme park visit turning into a nightmare none of them could comprehend. Adult responses ran the gamut of being fearfully calm while organizing their family to outright screaming and crying as their imminent death seemed to be hurdling at them.

Kevin took control of the aircraft, adjusting the trim wheel and handling the foot pedals to keep the gliding behemoth on course for the two bodies of water in front of him.

Lake Conway, and its sister Little Lake Conway sat ahead. With the 25-knot wind gusting in his face, his airspeed began to taper off.

"I'm reading 170 knots," Landrey said. "We are at 1800 feet and descending."

"Count down from 1000," Kevin shot back. "Let me know when we reach 130 knots."

With a water landing, Captain Stillwagon had to keep his landing gear up. If he was to attempt an emergency landing on solid ground, dropping the landing gear would give him some last minute speed reduction and a bit more control over where he set down. But if the gear were dropped now, it would grab the water and flip the aircraft over and likely break the plane into pieces.

"Are those lakes long enough to bring us down?" Landrey asked.

The A320 needs a minimum of 6000 feet of runway to land, and the lakes in front of them looked to be just short of that, at least in the direction they were travelling.

"They are not quite a mile wide, but we don't need that much for a water landing!" Kevin replied. "500 yards should get us down and floating."

The A320, when brought down intact and under control, could float for almost an hour. Chesley Burnett "Sully" Sullenberger had done an identical maneuver in the Hudson River back in 2009. His U.S. Air flight 1549 Airbus A320 floated long enough that the only injury or damage any of the passengers suffered was wet shoes as they walked off the wing of the aircraft into the emergency boats that had been dispatched. Kevin loved that story and was grateful that he had a chance of repeating "Sully's miracle on the Hudson." If only his airspeed could hold out, they could have a chance at walking away from the mess they were in.

"Airspeed down to 130, boss." The First Officer said.

"Damn," Kevin replied. "That headwind is knocking us down hard!"

"Altitude 1000," Tyler replied.

Kevin watched his airspeed rapidly bleed away. They were coming up on the southern lake, Lake Conway, and it was going to be close. Real close. The ground and trees were rapidly coming up to meet them. Sitting at the front of the metal missile he had control over just a minute ago used to be exhilarating. Now, with minimal control, the windshield seemed little protection and watching the landscape rapidly expand and rush up to meet him made him regret the panoramic view he was seeing.

"I don't think we're going to make it!" the co-pilot shouted.

Kevin had just a few seconds left and the trees were coming up at him more quickly than he had hoped. It was looking more and more like they were going to come up short.

"500 feet," Perkins said solemnly. "400, 350, 300, 250, 200."

As the final seconds ticked away, Kevin could see that the tree line was going to get to them before the water. The headwind was strong and their airspeed had gone down rapidly. He checked his trim wheel and found he had a bit more he could drop it. He spun the wheel drum back, dropping the trim tab down as far as it could go, raising the nose of the aircraft a few more feet. He had done all he could and as the altimeter read 100, he saw that they were just short. The tree tops loomed in front of him, rushing at the window like a freight train. He said a quick prayer and thought of his wife and daughter. They weren't going to make it!

Lake Conway Estates

Jorge loved his house. Raised in Orlando by a poor Mexican immigrant family, his father had a small landscape company and his mother worked housekeeping at Disney World. He grew up in a large Catholic family with four brothers and three sisters. With the help of their church, they all went to St. John Vianney Catholic School. Private high school was financially out of the question so the eight children all attended Oak Ridge High School where he excelled in both baseball and academics, taking AP classes in English, Calculus and Psychology. Jorge was one of seven out of eight siblings to get a Bachelor's degree or higher. He attended Rollins College in Winter Park on a partial baseball scholarship, just a few miles from where he grew up in Southeast Orlando. He worked his way through school getting jobs bussing tables and cutting lawns. It was hard work but like most students that had to work for their education, he rose to the top of his abilities. Jorge walked out of college with a degree from one of the finest business schools in the southeast United States. Within eight years, he had risen to vice-president of an international bank where his finance degree brought him a well-deserved position and salary.

Today, Jorge Vasquez walked out onto the deck of his house that overlooked Lake Conway. He had purchased the home earlier that year from a foreclosure list at the bank and now at 30 years old, he stood next to the lake, drinking a well-deserved beer, proudly looking over the back yard where a boy from poor Mexican immigrants had made it to a level that his parents could not even dream of. He thought of the years at Rollins where rich kids from rich parents sent their children to get a rich-man's education. It was a ticket into a club where the wealthy took care of each other. The education was top notch and the company he kept was thick with money and prestige. Jorge never really fit in with most of them. Not that they weren't nice enough to him, but there was always an undercurrent to their relationships. When your classmates were named Chip, Matt and Craig, the name Jorge never really seemed to fit. But Jorge didn't hate them, it just all seemed too easy for his fellow classmates. It's not like it was their fault being born into wealth, but Jorge knew he deserved to be where he was. He had earned it.

With the stock market closing at 4 p.m., Jorge slipped out of the office after finishing his reports. His drive to the new house took less than 20 minutes. He relaxed with a cold beer, thinking about tonight's plans. He was meeting his latest girlfriend, Maria. She was the first Latino he had dated since graduating from college. His dark complexion, deep brown eyes and athletic physique really got him any woman he wanted. The past eight or nine years found him with various girlfriends, all of which you could classify as wealthy and blonde.

Maria, on the other hand, was from a family his parents knew. Jorge had decided to get serious about his private life. The idea of having a wife and children were now starting to poke at his subconscious mind. His mother had been bugging him for years, but like many things in life, it all came down to timing. Now was the time as far as Jorge was concerned. His co-workers were mostly married and a couple of his fellow vice-presidents were working on their first kids. Maria, to date, had been everything he could ask for and more. Tonight they were going to dine downtown with couples from his bank. It was to be the first introduction Maria would have into his business life. He knew she would be a hit. She was intelligent and successful, just like Jorge.

As he gazed over the water, there was a growing feeling of something Jorge just couldn't quite comprehend. A thought or an awareness was gnawing at him that things were wrong. He pulled his phone out of his pocket to look at the time and he saw that it had died.

"Damn," he said to the phone. "I thought I charged you."

Jorge turned to go back into his house when he felt a presence descend over him. In a flash, he could feel a pressure that was overwhelming. He realized suddenly that the world was eerily quiet, almost like a tomb. In a fraction of a second, his athletic instincts told him that something was dramatically wrong. He remembered the same feeling from high school. Although a standout in baseball, Jorge played football as a defensive back. Once, he remembered defending the opponent's wide receiver on a deep fly route to the end zone. There was a moment when he heard the crowd roar and he knew that the ball was in the air and coming his way and he now had that same sinking feeling. That's when he knew something was wrong. There was no noise. Nothing at all. Normally, cars could be heard whisking along the road nearby. The only sounds he heard now was a lone mockingbird blasting out its call.

Then, a building presence of what he could only describe as a wave of air began to quickly grow, and a low, deep rumble was coming from the front of his new home. Jorge stood looking at the back of his house, wondering what could possibly make such a deep and frightening noise, when he saw the nose of a huge jet plane cresting over his roofline. It enveloped the sky above him as it majestically crossed over his head, seemingly touching the top of his house. He could almost reach up and brush the bottom of the aircraft as it passed over his head and dropped out of the sky. He was too stunned to move as the magnificent beast blasted through the vegetation behind his beautiful lakefront home.

Just as quickly as it passed overhead, the jumbo jet was through the copse of trees that lined the water, gliding toward the opposite side of the lake. The engines hanging from each wing miraculously cut through the live oaks that hugged the edge of the water, cutting a swath of small branches and leaves and leaving behind a hole in the canopy above. Jorge ran to the water's edge as the enormous metal bird slowly descended towards the surface of the lake. It was a sight he would never forget, especially since he didn't know if the beast would come down in time to avoid smashing into the homes on the opposite shore.

Delta Flight 2181

Captain Stillwagon could hardly believe it. His jet passed through the canopy of trees and was lined up to settle down onto the lake underneath him. The big bird kept gliding over the water, seemingly afraid to touch the glassy surface. Kevin began to worry that we was overshooting the lake and would pancake the plane and all aboard into the houses on the rapidly approaching shoreline.

"Kevin!" the first officer shouted, pointing to the opposite shore.

"I KNOW!" he shouted back.

Captain Stillwagon spun his trim wheel forward, lowering the nose of the plane. It was a delicate maneuver. If he dipped too low, the nose of the craft would bury itself into the water and the tail would flip over in a somersault maneuver that would at the least, place the plane upside down. At the worst, and most likely, the plane would break apart.

The nose of the jet dipped toward the water, its nose down position dropping the jet more rapidly than before.

"Running out of room," Landrey shouted. "Half a mile to the shore!"

Kevin flew by feel, finally spinning the trim wheel back when he felt that the jet was ready to settle into the lake. As the nose started to rise, the plane contacted the water. First it skipped a bit, until it settled enough to have the engines grab and drag them to a rapid stop. From contact with the water to its final position floating in the lake, the jet traveled just over 300 yards, about half the normal emergency stopping distance seen on land.

The passengers and crew had been thrown forward when the engines caught the water, but the incessant screaming by the flight attendants to "bend over and keep your heads down" had resulted in most passengers having little more than a black and blue mark across their wastes.

Kevin exhaled. He realized he hadn't taken a breath for the past minute. He looked back to his right to examine the wings. The craft was floating! As he was looking out the right, Landrey leapt from his seat and stared out his left side window, and began to laugh.

"Check it out, Skipper!" he giggled as he pointed out the left side of the windshield.

"Tell the flight attendant to have them depart the plane on the left!"

Kevin leaned over to his co-pilot's side and smiled. The left wing was there, butting up against a dock that sat on the northern shore of the lake. The passengers were already flowing out onto the wing, the emergency exit having been opened. The first of his "souls" tiptoed out onto the wooden dock and waved back at the cockpit. Kevin closed his eyes and said a prayerful thanks.

First officer Landrey opened the door to the cockpit as Kevin got on the overhead phone.

"Ladies and gentlemen. This is the termination of flight 2181, La Guardia to Orlando. Please exit out the left side emergency door and make your way to the dock at the end of the wing. This is Captain Stillwagon thanking you for flying Delta Airlines!"

The cabin erupted in a deafening cheer. Landrey looked back at Kevin and smiled.

"Nice job, Sully!"

The two of them waited for the passengers to disembark the plane, making sure to check the aircraft before leaving themselves. They were the last people off the ship.

All were ashore within 10 minutes, but were confronted with yet another problem. No one had a working cell phone. Kevin smiled and patted Tyler on the shoulder.

"What a day," he said. "At least the worst is over."

Little did he know!

CHAPTER 7

Day 1

Charlie

Kirkman Specialty Clinic

Four of us left the office and walked down the road to the local Publix supermarket. Two of them were new to the practice but thankfully, Janice joined our group. She and I were about the same age and had spoken at length a few times over the past year. She was sweet, and as southern as you could get. She was from Alabama.

As expected, the store was just as dark as all the other buildings we had passed. We went up to the sliding electronic front doors that had been manually pushed aside. A young man held up his hand to prevent us from entering. A crowd of customers sat in the parking lot, grimly checking their phones and sitting on the hoods of their cars.

"Sorry, closed." He said in a terse voice. "Electricity is out and we can't let anyone in."

"We're from Dr. Kramer's office," I said. "Are you Mr. Wayneright?"

"No," he replied. "He's in the back."

I looked back into the store and I could see flashlight beams crisscrossing the aisles. *Well, at least they worked*, I thought.

"Look," I said with a smile. "Could you go get him? I would really appreciate it if you could do that for us."

"I'm sorry, but Mr. Wayneright is busy. We have to tape up the freezer doors and coolers so the food doesn't spoil. He can't break away now."

I continued to prod the young man, pleading with him to just reconsider. I tried to reason with him, beg him and even flirt with him. Seeing that I am a poor flirter, I didn't get far with that.

Janice was standing behind me, listening to the conversation. She quietly turned around and unbuttoned her lab jacket. She fussed with something under her scrub top and quickly pulled out her bra. Her scrubs were tight to begin with, and once her bra was gone, her chest swelled out and made the top even tighter. Her cleavage was barely contained by the stiffened material. She stuffed her bra into her lab coat and slung the coat across her forearm. She did a little primping with her hair and eased into position next to my right shoulder.

"Oh… Please…" she said with a thick, honey-laced southern accent. "We have patients that are just suffering at our office. I know the doctor has check writing approval here. We brought a check; or you could add it all up and send the bill with me. Then we can just go back and help those poor souls." She gently bit her lower lip when she finished and gave him a kitten-like smile. *That was so over the top*! I thought. *He's going to have us escorted out of the parking lot.*

Until that moment, I never appreciated the power that an unleashed pair of breasts had over a young, heterosexual man. The poor kid never had a chance. He never raised his eyes above her neck.

"Ah… sure." He stammered. "I'll go check." He spun around and entered the darkened building.

"Holy crap!" I said to Janice. "I never thought that would work."

"You'd be surprised," she said. "More times than not."

"Well you have more to work with than I do," I replied.

"Honey," she said as she worked her southern accent again. "It's not the size. It's the promise of what's past the fabric that holds their attention!"

We both laughed as Janice put her lab coat back on, covering herself once again.

Within a minute, Mr. Wayneright came to the door.

"Sir," I said. "Dr. Kramer asked me to speak to you directly. He gave me a list of things he needs at the office right away. He said you could help."

"Sure," he said in a hushed voice. "Go around back and I'll let you in. I can't have the others outside see that I'm making an exception for you. Just go around to the right and I'll meet you at the loading dock."

He left, and the poor lust-struck boy returned to guard the door. Janice slid up next to him and gave him a kiss on the cheek, making sure to press her chest lightly against his.

"You are the sweetest thing," she cooed.

As we started walking down the sidewalk and around the building, she looked over at me, smiled and said, "You never know when I might need him again."

"So why is Mr. Wayneright so accommodating?" I asked.

"Dr. Kramer saved his dad," Janice said simply. "He did a coronary CT scan based on some obscure symptoms and found an aortic aneurism. His dad had emergency surgery that day. If Dr. Kramer hadn't found the ballooning blood vessel, it would have ruptured and Mr. Wayneright's father would have died instantly. I don't think any other cardiologist could have put those symptoms together and ordered that scan."

"That's why I like the man," I replied. Everyone just nodded their heads as we rounded the corner and saw the open door.

Mr. Wayneright turned out to be the store manager. He led us into the darkened store and looked at the list the doctor had made. Most of the items were canned and dried food. He also had us shop for over the counter medical supplies like Band-Aids, Advil and Tylenol as well as a lot of feminine products. I wasn't sure why those were important. We filled up four carts to the brim and rolled them to the loading dock. Mr. Wayneright estimated the cost of the haul and Janice filled out a signed blank check. He gave us a written receipt, and we rolled our carts by the back of the building and out onto the highway. We managed to avoid the prying eyes of the people in the parking lot and made it back to the office without incident. There were a lot of raised eyebrows as we sauntered down the thoroughfare. It really felt strange to walk in the middle of the street pushing a shopping cart, bypassing idled cars and trucks that should be traveling at over 40 miles per hour.

We were unloading the items in the break room when Dr. Kramer came in to see if we had accomplished our mission.

"We're back, and Mr. Wayneright said to say hello," Janice said.

"Looks like you've gotten everything," he happily replied.

"Sure did," Janice shot back. "But I was wondering what these backpacks are for?"

Dr. Kramer had us pick up any backpacks that were available. There were three black ones left in the school supply section and we grabbed them all. They were more book bags than backpacks; so we took them, given no other good options.

"They're for the future," he replied without further explanation, and he left the room. We all just stood and stared at each other, none of us knowing quite what he was talking about.

The next few hours were mostly boring. A couple of people from the street made their way to the office, but Dr. Kramer told them to wait with their cars. We brought a hose out to the side of the building and provided water to any that wanted it; but by the evening, most had wandered off to wherever they could find shelter. A hotel down the street soon filled to capacity while most folks started to walk home. By midnight, the street was mostly clear and we settled down to get some sleep.

Dr. Kramer had us wash out and fill as many containers with water as we could find. Trash bins and kitchen pots were sterilized and used to hold water. We kept them in one of the surgical suites. Every sink was sealed with plastic wrap and surgical tape, then filled to capacity. Dr. Kramer explained that the water pressure would likely give out as the theme parks and hotels nearby drained them.

I settled down next to Janice on the floor of the reception area. Along with the waiting room, it was one of the few areas with carpet. The rest of the building was covered with surgical tile to enhance sterility in those areas. I fell asleep sometime after 2 a.m., awakening several times as people about me snored or shifted to find a comfortable position. I lived by myself, and other than an occasional overnight guest, I slept alone. All those bodies moving about prevented any significant rest.

CHAPTER 8

Day 1

Officer John Drosky

East Orlando

It was dark by the time John got back to his patrol car just a block down the road. The past couple of hours had been a mixture of hope and frustration. John watched strangers perform noble and kind deeds for each other under extraordinary circumstances. Others, gratefully a minority, seemed to descend into a primal need to lash out at others, taking or bullying anyone to get what they wanted. With the power out, the gas station and 7/11 on the block had closed. With no electricity to power the pumps, run the register or credit card reader, it was best for them to simply close up shop. But the owners or workers were stuck there. Most just sat in the door to their stores, letting the outside air keep them cool on the warm, November day.

In one instance, two men tried to force themselves into a local gas-and-go convenience store. The two lowlifes had pulled out an old revolver on the owner who was sitting in the doorway of the store, but didn't realize that his son was standing behind him with a Mossberg 500 shotgun. Although no shots were fired, John recognized the rapid societal deterioration that was taking place. It was easy to be charitable when you thought the power would be back on in a few hours. It was a different matter to give when you weren't going to be able to replenish what little you had left. It was going to get nasty soon.

John's OPD uniform was a magnet for each and every person that he came across. Hundreds of people surrounded him with questions about the loss of power and demands that he do something about it (like he could actually turn the power back on). It reinforced his belief that people were totally dependent on the government and society was only three days without power away from total anarchy. If the first few hours were any indication, fighting insurgents in Fallujah might actually look good compared to what he could expect in Orlando a week from now.

John had been in the Marines before entering the police academy. He had use the Delayed Entry Program (DEP) when he turned 18 during his senior year at Colonial High School, becoming a "poolee" until basic training was completed the following summer. His four year enlistment contract ended while he was deployed in Afghanistan. His time in the 1/3 out of Hawaii included two months of intense door-to-door fighting in Fallujah where he lost several close friends to IEDs and sniper fire. The rest of the Anbar province proved almost as difficult but he performed well, earning a number of ribbons and medals including the Bronze Star with Valor and Purple Heart. That was 2004, just a year after he had been sworn into the Corps. At the end of his four year term of enlistment he decided to enter civilian life and found his calling in with the Orlando Police Department.

The training to become an officer took almost five months of full-time study at the local community college. With his military service record and top of the class grades, he was quickly hired by the city. Although many days brought some frustrations, most of the time, John felt like he was making a difference. Most people were grateful for his work and it was not uncommon for strangers to come up and shake his hand and thank him for being a cop. However, in a few days, his uniform was going to become a magnet for frustration and anger as people realized that the government had failed to protect them at the most basic level. Without food, water or power, citizens were going to become a lynch mob, and as unfair as that seemed, John knew he would be at the end of that rope. *Yep*, he thought, *I need to get rid of this uniform.*

John decided that his best move was to hunker down in the young man's house for the night to see how things fleshed out. The walk to headquarters would only take him a few hours, but to what end? If airliners were falling out of the sky, there was no doubt that this was at least a regional event and probably not limited to the Orlando area. If electricity from other parts of the country could be diverted to Florida, he might see a restoration of the city's power within a few days. His apartment was at the other end of the city and if he needed to, John felt he could make it there in a day's walk. Right now, he needed to rest and regroup. It had been a hell of a day.

John re-entered the house. The bodies in the back bedroom needed to be left undisturbed in case forensics found their way here. It would be another day before they started to smell, and he doubted he would be here that long. John shut the bedroom door, entombing the two women if or until someone came to collect evidence. Either way, it wasn't his problem anymore.

He went back to his patrol car and stripped it of anything of value. He collected his standard issue Remington 870P shotgun and extra ammunition for both the shotgun and his 9mm Sig. A level IIIA bullet resistant tactical vest with OPD stenciled across the front came along. The first-aid and tool-kit, flashlight and batteries along with a hand held radio were also scavenged. Lastly, his personal backpack with a change of clothing and some work-out wear for the gym were all taken into the house. John searched about in the drawers and located some candles and several lighters.

Soon, he had the kitchen lit up, and he began to create a Bug out Bag out of his 5.11 backpack. One of the benefits of being active duty law enforcement was the discounts from tactical supply stores. His backpack, normally costing over 150 dollars, came with a 40% discount. With eight years under his belt, he was close to making almost 70 thousand dollars a year. When he first started with O.P.D. and was earning just over 30k, the discount meant so much more.

John divided the food into two groups, those that would spoil without power, and those items that would last a while. Having separated the food into two groups, he further divided the long-term food into two more sets. High calorie, light weight (HCLW) items and the rest. The HCLW items were set aside for his backpack. They included the standard items like peanut butter, candy, seven protein bars, 12 instant oatmeal packs and a half a jar of Planter's peanuts among other items. Everything that could be transferred into a zip lock bag was moved into plastic and sealed. Jars or other breakable items and cans were abandoned. His only allowance for a jar was the peanut butter. He limited his metal containers to two cans of spam, three cans of tuna and a bunch of Underwood Deviled Ham spread (a nice find with 360 calories per can; Half of the calories were carbs while the other half were fat and protein).

He opened the refrigerator and quickly removed the few items he found. He was surprised at the lack of food for what should have been three people, but found a half a pound of bologna, half a loaf of bread and some cheese and mustard. He managed to make five sandwiches and bagged them before putting them in the freezer, most of its space taken up by a couple of bottles of vodka. He pulled them out and consolidated them into one bottle before replacing the alcohol back into the freezer. It would, at least, act as a temperature reservoir to keep the sandwiches cold for as long as possible.

When he was finally finished, and if he was careful, he figured he had about a week's worth of calories in his backpack.

With that task completed, John decided to load up on calories from the food that would spoil over the next day or two. Cereal and milk, a Tupperware container of some kind of stew (not bad, actually) and ice cream made up his late night dinner. One of the things he had learned was that if you weren't going to be able to eat in the future, best to load up on the calories while you could. By the time Officer Drosky had finished, he felt like he was going to puke.

He made his way into the bathroom, and grateful that the water still flowed and should be relatively clean, he stripped off his uniform and took a long shower. He scrubbed and shampooed and luxuriated in the hot, steamy water until he felt the temperature rapidly turn cold. With a sigh, he shut the water off, not knowing when a hot shower would ever come his way again.

Having enjoyed the shower, he dried off and remembered to add some bleach for water purification and dish soap to his bag. Small containers in the garage were cleaned out and two of them were filled with the disinfecting liquids. He had to plan for the long term, although where that would be was yet to be seen.

John found the couch, and blowing out all the candles save one, he got a pillow from one of the other bedrooms, along with a bed throw and spare sheets. He put his Sig 226 on the coffee table next to him and lay back, reflecting on the day and what the future held.

His lack of a committed relationship, originally a sad side-effect of his job, now seemed to be a benefit. Every year, he would find or be introduced to a nice girl. At first, things would go well, but after a few months, the job would get in the way. His first few years were often nightshifts and weekends; not the best hours to foster a relationship with women working 9 to 5. However, the past year found him with more and more day-hours and weekdays, a benefit of his increasing seniority. Now, just past 30-years old, John felt that the timing was right for a committed relationship. Unfortunately, finding the right match had gotten more and more difficult. Most of the single women were single for a reason. Not that John minded a hard-working woman, but the many dates he had been on over the past few years had not gone too well. Recently, the women he had dated were usually pushing thirty as well and tended to be married to their jobs. John wanted a more old-fashioned marriage, one where he would be working while his wife could stay home, hopefully putting her energy into a family and not punching a time-card or working late for a bonus check. It was starting to worry him that the women he was now meeting were not interested in children, but rather in their careers. On top of that, many of the women he had dated more than once turned out to want the thrill of dating a cop rather than wanting to find a committed relationship. John's Polish heritage had given him the tall, Slavic look that a lot of women found attractive. His blue eyes and swarthy dark hair looked especially good when he had not shaved for a day or two. So as nice as it was, sex wasn't a problem. Unfortunately, John wanted more than that but had found that most of the "good ones" had already begun their lives with someone other than him. He was worried that he may have missed his chance between his four years as a Marine and the next six to eight years of O.P.D. putting him on the street all those nights and weekends.

Now, as he lay in the candle-lit living room, he was grateful he didn't have anyone to worry about. His parents were dead, both passing within the last four years. He had been an "oops" baby, coming when his parents had given up hope of having a child. His mother was over forty when he was born and his father pushing fifty. When his mom died of ovarian cancer four years ago, his father lost his will to stick around and passed soon after. John devoted himself to his work after that, it was all he had. Now, it seemed to be a blessing.

As he drifted off to sleep, he heard a distant crack of gunfire. Knowing that it was many blocks away, he was grateful that he didn't have anyone to worry about. It made falling asleep a little easier and he blew out the candle. A surprisingly deep and rested sleep found him a minute later while the rest of the city began a slow burn towards its eventual demise.

CHAPTER 9

Day 1

Holding Cell, 33rd Street Jail

The young man dozed in a fitful slumber while leaning against the wall of the holding cell. His new burn marks were starting to become both painful and exhausting at the same time. His skin had been scorched many times in the past three years and like most painful or stressful things, a person's tolerance became almost non-existent with each successive assault. He didn't want to have to tolerate the pain anymore. It was what made him snap that morning and it was keeping him from finding any comfort at the moment.

He could hear the other prisoners murmuring amongst themselves, but he tried his best to look within himself and ignore the others. The smell of body odor from his fellow inmates and urine near the open toilet made for an interesting aroma. The aura of the others nearby left him wanting to leave, a feeling he hadn't felt since the whole ordeal began.

Sticking the knife into his mother's girlfriend hadn't phased him in the least. She was a monster, and monsters deserved to die. His mother, on the other hand… now that was starting to become a gnawing headache in the back of his brain.

In truth, the death of his mother had been coming for years. She had become increasingly bitter as the years with her girlfriend passed. Several times in the first few years after the divorce, she had attempted to resolve things with his dad. But each time, his father had rejected her attempts at reconciliation.

The first time was when she lost her permanent alimony. The

girlfriend's attorney had assured her that she would be "set for life" since permanent alimony would never end unless she remarried. It was all his mother needed to file for divorce and live the exciting life her girlfriend promised. She would never have to marry again, and what woman receiving permanent alimony would every remarry when she could just live with their boyfriend or girlfriend and enjoy a lifetime of welfare? But when the final divorce decree came down, his mother only was given temporary, rehabilitative alimony. She immediately tried to reunite with his dad, but he recognized her true motivations and refused.

The second time she tried to reconcile with his father was when her girlfriend had beaten her. Again, his dad denied her, figuring she had made her bed, now she could sleep in it. His mom eventually agreed to go back to her girlfriend if she promised not to beat her anymore. That was when the boy started to become the punching bag, taking his mother's place. That was three years and seven broken ribs ago.

So the boy was conflicted when he thought of shoving the knife into his mother's chest. No matter what she had allowed, and participated in, she was still his mother. It was hurtful that she let him be beaten, bruised and burnt. So when she herself had crossed the line that morning and started choking the young man, she received the six inch blade for her efforts. But despite her abuse, it was still his mother.

His OCD was starting to kick in and the snakes and spiders that felt like they were crawling on his skin were starting to make their presence known. So he began to count the tiles on the ceiling to occupy his time and take his mind off of his building stress. Soon, his skin settled down and he started to feel the tightness in his chest abate.

"Hey boy," he heard. "Whatcha in for?" One of the others asked.

The young man barely heard the question, continuing his ritualistic ceiling tile counting, not wanting to have to start over if he lost his concentration. The others continued their murmuring and then it got quiet. The boy had just finished counting the third row of tiles when he felt a jolt to his left shoulder. Someone had hit him in one of the burn marks and he let out a yelp. Standing in front of him was a tall, lanky man who desperately needed a shave and shower. His teeth, the few he had left, were covered in a plaque of yellow and brown crust that seemed to be holding them together, each of his lower front teeth tilting at an impossible angle. The man didn't look much past 40 years old, but his skin and teeth told a story of a very hard life. The tattoos on his upper body bled out of the neck-line of his t-shirt, hinting of a well inked torso beneath. His head had been shaved bald. If he had been a woman, he would have been described as *ridden hard and put away wet*. As it was, he didn't like the kid ignoring him and the punch to his shoulder brought the boy back to reality.

The man looked back at the others, searching for approval. He turned his attention back to the boy and glared at the youth, sizing him up like a lion would do to a gazelle.

"I said," he hissed. "What are you doing in here?"

The boy, well beyond caring, simply shrugged and continued to rub the burn that had just been punched.

"Are you stupid?" The man continued. "What are you doing in here?"

The boy started at his tormentor, watching as the man constantly glanced back over his shoulder at the others. That's when he noticed the other man. Also shaved bald, this one had an air about him that reeked of authority. This one stared back at him, his eyes boring through the boy's gaze leaving no doubt who was in charge.

"Come on, punk!" The man in front of him said as he clenched his fist for another strike. "We want to know what a white bread kid like you is doin' in the cell with us! Now TALK! What are you charged with?"

The young man relented. He looked down at the floor and whispered to the man.

"Murder," he said in a low voice.

"Murder my ass!" The man chortled. "You ain't murdered no one."

The boy continued to stare at the floor as the man stood his ground in front of him.

"OK, White Bread." He continued. "Who'd you put down? Just who did you off? Your teacher? Was she giving you bad grades? Come on! Tell me, just who did you kill? Mr. Big, Bad Man!"

"My mom," he whispered back.

The verbal assault ended. His assailant stepped back and turned to the others. The leader, a big man with even more tattoos than the first one stepped forward. He moved with a grace that belied his size. As he approached, the boy could make out the tattoos with even greater detail. Several swastikas were evident as well as an Iron Cross. The number 88 was stenciled on his right cheek while the number 14 was stenciled on the left one. His blue eyes bore into the young man as he stepped up. He crouched in front of the boy and reached out, lifting his chin to stare into his eyes. The man, the leader of the group, spoke.

"Why?"

The boy, unsure why he should answer, simply lifted his shirt and the man and his minion stared at his scarred and burned chest.

The leader shook his head up and down, and letting go of the boy's chin, lifted his own shirt up, revealing the pucker marks of his own burnt and scarred torso. The leader turned to the others and pronounced "He's one of ours now! Protect him."

Then he turned back to the boy. "Name's Taurus," he said. "You're now protected by the Aryan Brotherhood. You'll be safe."

And with that, the lights went out.

CHAPTER 10

Day 2

Charlie

Kirkman Specialty Clinic

About 6 a.m. the next morning I had had enough of my tossing and turning. Most of the people still slumbered, and the morning sun had not yet risen. I got up and found Dr. Kramer in the break room, making a large pot of coffee in an old percolator. I saddled up next to him and found two clean mugs. I knew where most of the utensils were stored given the multiple lunches I had brought on my frequent sales calls to the office. We both worked in silence as we reflected on the situation and unsuccessfully sought a solution to our predicament. It's very calming preparing your morning cup of coffee, almost Zen-like.

We sat down at the table and enjoyed our cup of java. After a minute of welcome silence, he put his mug down and we began to speak.

"Do you have any other clothes?" He asked.

"I have my workout clothes in my backseat," I cautiously replied. "Why?"

"Do you have gym shoes as well?"

"Well, yeah! They're running shoes." I said. "I usually hit the gym on my way home. But why are you worried about that?"

"I think you'll need those shoes, and your workout clothes. I think we can even scrounge up some scrubs for you."

"Whoa!" I said. "I'm not staying here that long."

"You may not have a choice," he flatly replied. "I haven't heard a single siren or other emergency vehicle all night. Have you?"

"Come to think of it," I said back. "No. No I haven't."

"Then it's worse than a local problem. It has to be at least city-wide or greater."

He got up and refilled his mug, adding a bit of sugar and powdered creamer before returning to the table.

"Charlie," he started. "Let me tell you what's going to happen over the next few weeks."

I started to interrupt him, fully intent on setting him straight. I was not going to stay here that long. No way! No how! But before I could get a word in, he held up his hand to shush me. He was Dr. Kramer, so I shut up and listened.

"Charlie, the world as you know it is going to fall apart. And I don't mean fall apart like a hurricane or tornado hit us. I mean, fall apart like the world is going to end."

I couldn't believe what he was saying. If it had been anyone but him, I would have left the table and never come back, writing him off as a quack. But his eyes and demeanor told me that he wasn't fooling around. He was dead serious, and I held his gaze and just kept quiet.

"Do you have any place to go that is safe? Before you answer that, I mean safely away from the city or other large crowds of people."

I thought of all my relatives and friends. I tried to think of someone that lived in a rural area, maybe on a farm or in the country. I came up blank.

"Not really, doctor." I replied. "My father lives in Maitland and my mom is in Tampa. All my friends live downtown or in Baldwin Park."

"Hmmm," he said. "We'll have to think on this a bit."

We heard a sound outside the door and Janice shuffled in and joined us.

"Can you spare some coffee?" She asked.

"You know you don't need to ask," he replied.

Janice poured herself a large mug of coffee, added a yellow pack of sweetener and plopped next to me at the table. We waited for her to take a couple of sips before we started back into the conversation.

"I want you both to understand what we are facing here," he began again. "We are looking at months or possibly years without power."

Janice and I both looked at each other. What he was saying was unfathomable. How could he be so certain?

"You both know I was in the Air Force, right?"

We nodded our heads in unison.

"I have some experience with this scenario. We were trained on the potential effects of an EMP attack. Now I'm not saying there has been an attack on the United States," he continued, "but regardless of the cause, the results are the same."

"If what I remember is correct, it may take months or years to re-establish electric power and normal utilities. Large population centers like Orlando are not going to fare well. When people run out of food and water, they will go searching, and with no police, it's going to get ugly."

I shuddered at his words, and hesitated to ask the next obvious question but Janice beat me to it.

"How bad is it going to get?" She asked.

"As bad as you can imagine," he replied. "And worse."

We sat silently for a minute, neither Janice nor I could comprehend what he was saying.

"Janice," he continued. "Do you have any friends or relatives that live outside Orlando? Preferably in a rural or farm setting?"

"Well," she replied. "My sister lives in DeLand. It's not really farm country, but she and her husband have a home on about five acres of land out east of the town. It's pretty isolated."

"Good," he exclaimed. "Then you need to get there when the time comes."

"How will we get there?" She asked. "My car doesn't work and there are no busses running to DeLand. Heck, there isn't anything running at all."

"You're going to have to walk," he simply stated. "Unless you have a bike, then you can ride there."

"You're kidding!" She said. "You're pulling my leg."

"I wish I was," he replied. "In fact, I want you to be able to leave on a moment's notice. That's why I had you pick up some backpacks yesterday. You'll need them."

"This is just ridiculous," she shot back. "There's no way I can walk 35 miles to my sister's house. It would take days."

"Possibly," he replied. "But if I'm right, you won't have much of a choice."

"I don't know," I interjected. "I run at least five miles a day. If you walked at a good pace you could be there in just over 24 hours."

"That brings up my next suggestion," he said. "Do you think you could take Charlie with you? It would be best if you travelled as a pair."

"I don't want to leave here," Janice finally confessed. "We have electricity and food. Why should I leave?"

"Because," he stated, "It's going to get violent soon. Very violent. People will turn on each other when they have nothing to eat. Most of the stores in the area only carry a two or three-day supply of food. When people realize that the government isn't coming to the rescue, they will do what they must to feed themselves and their families. Once the stores are cleared out, there will be rioting and a lot of violence. Worse of all, criminals will realize that the police won't be around. There's nothing stopping them from committing any crime they want, no matter how atrocious or vile. You don't want to be here when that happens."

"What are you going to do?" I asked.

"I don't have any choice," he replied. "I have to stay here. I have almost a dozen patients that need to be taken care of. If I leave, they have no chance."

"But if what you're saying is true," I countered, "if you stay, you will die."

"Possibly," he simply stated. "But I can't leave them here alone. It's not who I am. I will stay until we are rescued or I'm no longer needed."

The implication that he would stay until the patients had expired shook me to the bone. What kind of man would stay and risk his life on such a hopeless cause? *He would,* I thought as I stared back at this amazing man. Right then, I decided to stay as long as I could help. Looking over at Janice, I saw the same determined look in her eyes too.

"I'm staying," I said. "And I think Janice is with me on this as well."

"Ditto, here." She replied. "I'm single too. My sister is the only one in the area."

Dr. Kramer tried to argue with us, but we simply excused ourselves from the table and went out to the reception area where our guests had begun to rise. We helped many to their feet, most of the patients being elderly and a couple of them rather weak. I counted 11 patients and 7 staff members, including Janice and me.

I went back to my car and retrieved my gym bag. I brought it back into the office and got out of my business suit. I changed into a borrowed set of scrubs and put on my running shoes. I felt a lot better getting out of my heels and into something comfortable. It helped my attitude greatly just having something comfy on my feet.

Dr. Kramer brought a fresh pot of coffee and a pitcher of water along with some breakfast items we had purchased the day before. After feeding our patients and arranging for their bathroom needs, he cornered the two of us.

"I know I can't make you leave," he said. "But I need you to plan on leaving quickly when the time arises. I need you to bring a backpack for each of you and meet me in my office in fifteen minutes."

He turned and beat a path down the hall before we could ask any questions. Fifteen minutes later, we entered his office and found him in a new set of scrubs with freshly washed hair.

"I have a shower in my private bathroom," he stated. "I want you to set up a schedule for the patients and staff to use the shower until the water shuts down. It won't matter how much we use now, we're a drop in the bucket compared to the hotels nearby. Please do that after we finish our conversation."

He grabbed our backpacks and we went into the break room. He opened our backpacks and began to fill it with bottled water and some of the food we got the day before.

"I want you to keep these packs in my office closet. After we fill them with food and water, I want you to get a spare set of scrubs and add them to the pack. I also want to set up a small medical pack."

He put six water bottles on the bottom of the pack and began to stuff dried food into it as well. He left out the canned goods to reduce the pack's weight.

"I figure you will each need a minimum of 2500 calories a day if you're walking and carrying some weight. I've loaded enough dried fruit, nuts and power bars for four days in each pack. There are a few pouches of Gatorade in there as well. Now let's see about making up a small med kit. Also, if you need it, grab any feminine product and a roll of toilet paper."

We raided the office's supply cabinet as well as some of the OTC purchases from the day before. Needless to say, after combining medications into one or two bottles, we had quite a pharmacy stuffed into a side pouch of the backpacks. Tylenol, Advil and Antibiotic ointments for cuts and scrapes. Gauze and other first aid items were encased in a Ziploc bag as well. We added a cheap flashlight we had picked up at Publix, and some baby wipes we had also bought. The grocery list was starting to make more sense.

Dr. Kramer left us, so we took the opportunity to find another set of scrubs that we could take as well. When he returned, he handed each of us two bottles. One was a sample bottle of Valium, the other a similar bottle of hydrocodone. Both contained five pills.

"What do we need these for?" I asked. "This is so illegal."

"I don't expect you will need them for yourselves. But you might find them useful if the need arises."

"What kind of need?" I asked, not understanding such a cryptic statement.

"For trade," he simply replied. "They might just save your life."

Janice and I looked at each other with an even deeper sense of fear. If Dr. Kramer was willing to risk his license, and possible jail time to give us these drugs, it was serious.

Dr. Kramer saw our expressions and gripped us both by our shoulders.

"Sorry for the bad pun I'm about to use," the cardiologist said. "But I'm as serious as a heart attack. You might need them in exchange for your freedom, or even your life."

I didn't know what to say. I was in shock, at least I thought I was until he asked one more question.

"Do either of you have a gun?"

Holy mother of God!

CHAPTER 11

Day 2

33rd Street Jail

"GUARD!" Taurus bellowed.

The corrections officer ignored the screams coming from the holding cell. All hell had broken loose when the power went out the prior night. Emergency lighting from the exit signs had provided some help for the first hour and a half, but those eventually died. With the air conditioning down, the jail became a giant sauna. Air failed to move and the body heat of over 4000 inmates sat stagnant within its walls. The oxygen in the building felt like it was being sucked away, making the guards and their charges even more uncomfortable. By morning, 12 of the inmates had passed out due to heat exhaustion.

Michael James Jones had become a corrections officer after high school. He was entering his third year with the Orange County Department of Corrections and until last night, had mostly enjoyed his job. Despite his youth (he was just 21 years old), he engendered a lot of respect from the prisoners. At almost six and a half feet tall, he towered over all but a rare few of the inmates and combined with heavy weight lifting, he presented a terrifying sight. He ignored Taurus' screams and turned to an approaching colleague.

"Hey Mikey!" One of the guards called out. "The warden's calling everyone into the cafeteria."

"Who's gonna keep an eye on these guys?"

"Captain says not to worry about it. Says were going to meet and figure out what to do with them all." The guard replied.

Jones shook his head and began to follow his coworker. As he strode down the hall, the prisoners became even more enraged. The only light in the hallway was coming from the officer's flashlight. He had already changed the batteries once using his personal penlight to put three new D-batteries into the Maglite flashlight. He used up the remainder of the batteries' life the night before using the high-beam setting to give the prisoners in his section as much light as possible. Now, he had the flashlight on economy mode. The 3D-battery flashlight should last over 100 hours on this setting, but the light it generated was a fraction of the high beam.

"Man, the power's been out for hours. What time is it? My phone died yesterday." Jones said.

"Mine too," his friend replied. "That's what the captain wants to talk about. It's spooky. Everyone's phones are dead. It doesn't make sense."

Some of the holding cells were small rooms with a solid steel door and shatterproof glass. Those had housed some of the more violent criminals. Late last night, they had been transferred into the common holding cells that had open bars which allowed air flow. Already, there had been several fights that had sent three inmates to the infirmary. They would live but all had multiple fractures. Leaving the prisoners packed into the cells didn't sit right with Jones, but with the power having been off for over 12 hours, nothing was sitting right with him at this point.

They made their way through various corridors and through locked doors that were now being manned by guards with keys rather than the electronic controlled locks. Each door had three corrections officers. All three carried live ammunition in their 9mm Smith and Wesson handguns as well as one officer carrying a Remington 870 pump action shotgun. Emergency lanterns sat on the floor and weapon mounted flashlights searched the hallway behind Jones for anyone who might not belong there. It was old school security now.

The two corrections officers made their way to the cafeteria and found a bench to sit on. Before they could finish greeting their fellow officers, the captain stepped on top of a table and began his speech.

"Gentlemen and ladies," he began. "This is no ordinary power outage."

And from there, it only got worse. Jones learned of the total loss of all electronics. Several officers had made their way outside and witnessed the shutdown of the city. Reports of aircraft falling from the sky and the lack of response by emergency personal anywhere reinforced the magnitude of the crisis.

"Our problem now is that we are losing our ability to keep the prisoners in their cells. Besides the obvious lack of air conditioning, the muffin monster is not functioning and we have sewage backups on the first floor."

"What's the muffin monster?" Jones whispered.

"It's the sewage grinder," one of the other officers whispered back. "When they send the piss and shit into the sewer system, it goes through a sewage grinder before its put into the city pipes. If the electricity stops, a backup generator kicks in. If that doesn't work, the crap backs up and comes back out the toilets and drains."

The captain continued to drone on and on, but the few salient points Jones picked up were simple and frightening. First, the power may not come back on for a long time, possibly weeks or months. Second, the prisoners were going to have to be let out of their cells and held outside the jail, but inside the double fence that surrounds the building. The captain didn't get into the details of the transfer, other than to say that all guards were to stay on duty until relief arrived. When that was, nobody knew.

Jones did some mental calculations as he made his way back to his post. It was already closing in on breakfast and getting light outside but no one had mentioned feeding the guards, let alone the prisoners. How 4000 criminals were to be guarded by a few hundred guards was beyond his paygrade. It didn't seem possible, but that was the brass' problem, not his. *My problem*, Jones thought, *is to stay alive...* and maybe find something to eat.

Captain Braddock stepped down from the table and strode back to the administrative side of the building. Two of the judges, Judges Bender and Hernandez had been stuck in the jail since yesterday afternoon. Both had been in the middle of arraignment hearings when the power died and both sat with open shirts and no shoes, trying to stay as cool as possible in the stifling heat.

"I don't see that we have a lot of choices here," Bender said to the room. "If this goes on for more than a few days, we'll have to let as many of the non-violent prisoners go as we can."

"I think we're jumping the gun a bit," Judge Hernandez replied.

"I wish we were," Captain Braddock retorted. "We've been through this already. There are no emergency protocols for this type of situation. We've most likely been hit with an EMP, and with the lack of anything electronic working at all, we have to prepare for the worse."

"We have printed records of the inmates and over 4000 of these records to go through." Bender said. "We need to start now and organize the prisoners into groups that can be processed if we have to start releasing them. It'll take several days to figure out who we can release and who we need to keep. We have to start now if we are going to be in any shape to make an informed decision. We have 48 hours to move the non-violent prisoners out and deal with the rest."

"Why 48 hours?" Braddock asked.

"While you were giving your little pep talk," Bender said. "We got word from the kitchen that we only have enough food for a week. If this thing goes on, we have to save as much of the food as we can for the guards and the worse of the prisoners that must stay incarcerated."

"I get it. If we can release the drug offenders and other non-violent prisoners," Hernandez continued, "we can stretch our supplies for a lot longer."

"This is impossible," Braddock shot back. "Where's the state government? Why hasn't the Sheriff done anything? What the hell is taking so long to fix things?"

"Captain," Judge Bender said with a slow shake of the head. "It may never get fixed."

CHAPTER 12

Day 2

Charlie

Kirkman Specialty Clinic

The following day wasn't much different at the office. We turned off all the lights and unplugged any electronic device that might still potentially be drawing power. We also consolidated all our important perishables into our medical refrigerator. By law, all medications or chemicals that need to be kept cold had to have their own refrigerator apart from a general purpose one. We kept the under-the-bar sized unit going in the sterilization area. We pulled out and discarded the few unneeded medicines that were in there and put in the food items we needed to preserve. With most of the cardiac dyes we used kept at room temperature, we lost little of value. We shut down the refrigerator in the break room and even turned off the water heater. With outside temperatures expected to stay in the high 80s for another day or two, the water was plenty warm enough.

Later in the evening though, we started to get an understanding of what Dr. Kramer was worried about. Down the street at the Publix, a large group of people had gathered, demanding to be let in. The grocery store was about a block or two away and on the other side of the street from the cardiology office. Janice and I decided to investigate what all the commotion was about, sneaking out the staff entrance.

After a block, we got a good look at the store. It wasn't a pretty sight.

From the looks of things, we could see Mr. Wayneright at the entrance. The few remaining employees had set up a table which blocked the front door. It looked like he was trying to organize the mob into a line. I moved closer to hear what he had to say.

"People!" He screamed. "We have enough for everyone. PLEASE! Just form a line to your left."

From what I could hear and see, the mob of several hundred was pressing up against the table and glass entrance windows. With the power out for more than a day, tempers were flaring although most were listening to instructions.

The savvy manager was distributing all the perishable items, including the frozen foods, meats and fresh fish. He was saving the canned and packaged items for later, hoping against hope that the power would return.

"HEY!" A rough looking man yelled. "WE NEED MORE THAN THIS!"

"YEAH!" Someone else yelled. "HOW AM I SUPPOSED TO HEAT UP A TV DINNER? NOTHING WORKS!"

Several "customers" at the front became agitated as the rear of the crowd pushed forward, worried they wouldn't be able to get their "fair share."

"PLEASE, PEOPLE!" the manager shouted. "IF YOU DON'T GET IN LINE, YOU WON'T GET ANYTHING. THERE IS PLENTY FOR EVERYONE!"

Some of the men in the crowd began to organize the group, and eventually some semblance of order was found and a line formed. As he began to distribute the food, problems began almost immediately. The first in line was a middle-aged woman dressed in a business suit and high heels. Her hair and makeup were a disaster. Without power for a hair dryer or lighting for a mirror, the facade of civilization was rapidly disappearing.

"Please," she uttered. "I need more than a couple of frozen dinners. I need personal supplies and cigarettes."

"I'm sorry, but this is all we can spare right now."

Others in the crowd heard her pleas, yelling at her to move along. Eventually, she relented and the second person in line moved up. When the man only received two items, he complained bitterly that he had a family at home. Mr. Wayneright relented and gave the man four items.

Mollified, he left and walked down the road towards Janice and me. As he passed, he turned to the two of us and muttered under his breath.

"It's shit over there," he said.

"What?" I asked.

The disheveled man stopped and looked at me with eyes that didn't look too sane.

"I said its shit down there. If you want anything, you better go now. This isn't going to last. That mob isn't going to listen to anyone for much longer."

With that, he turned and marched down the road towards a residential area about a mile away.

I turned to Janice, and we gave each other a knowing look. Dr. Kramer was right. Things were going to get out of hand real soon.

We continued to watch as the crowd slowly moved along. Mr. Wayneright began giving each person in line four items and things were proceeding remarkably well when a scuffle broke out as a woman passed through and received her share. Another woman in the crowd saw her and screamed that her husband had already been through once.

"SHE'S CHEATING!" The shrill woman yelled. "I KNOW HER. HER HUSBAND WENT THROUGH THE LINE ALREADY!"

The accuser pointed to a man standing to the side. From his reaction, it appeared that the accusation was true. The shrill woman jumped out of line and knocked the other woman down. She began to gather up the dropped groceries when the husband jumped into the fray. Within seconds, a dozen men jumped the husband and began to beat him mercilessly. He did his best to cover his face as blow after blow and kick after kick rained down. His food was stolen and the couple was left on the ground with nothing but pain and injuries for their troubles. The wife struggled over to her husband. He didn't move.

"My God," I said to Janice. "How can it get this bad this quick?"

Janice stood in shock. She started to go to the couple's aid when the husband slowly got himself to his feet and staggered to the back of the line once again. The wife sat on the ground sobbing. No one gave them comfort.

I grabbed Janice's arm and kept her from getting involved.

"This is just the first day," I whispered. "We need to get back and talk to Doctor Kramer."

She nodded silently and we retraced our steps back to the office. I was afraid. If this was what civilization was becoming and there was food still on the shelf, I wasn't looking forward to what the rest of the week would bring. We silently entered the side door and found Dr. Kramer in his office.

"Dr. Kramer," I said. "Janice and I went down to the Publix."

"Is it still there?" He replied. At first I thought he was joking, but then I looked into his eyes and saw he was dead serious.

"Yeah," I stammered.

"Well, I guess it has only been a day." He mused.

"I can't believe what we saw," Janice added. "People were like animals!"

"Was anyone killed?" He asked back.

"Well… no!" I replied.

"I'm surprised," he countered. "It won't be long now."

He smiled and got up, leaving the room to check on his patients. Janice and I sat in stunned silence. He was actually amazed that no one had been killed.

We didn't move for a while, and eventually Dr. Kramer returned from his "rounds" and sat heavily into his leather-backed chair.

"What are we going to do?" I asked.

"Go to DeLand," he simply replied.

"Not yet," I countered. "You still may need us."

He didn't respond. Instead he folded his hands together and placed them on his lap. Closing his eyes, he began to breathe heavily, and fell asleep. Like shutting off a light, he was alert and talking with us, and then he was out.

Janice and I quietly left and found our spot behind the front desk. We quickly made up our bed for the night. We lay silently next to each other, neither of us speaking, but unable to sleep. After a while, I felt myself drifting off when I heard three "pops" from outside. At first, I thought someone had set off firecrackers, but the first three were followed by two deeper booms. Gunfire!

I looked at Janice, both of us knowing that things had turned for the worse. I prayed that Mr. Wayneright was safe and grabbed Janice's left hand with mine. We held each other like that until I finally drifted off to sleep. For the first time in my life, I was afraid to wake up the next day.

CHAPTER 13

Day 3

Charlie

Kirkman Specialty Clinic

I awoke the next morning tired and short of patience. Another restless night and all we had to look forward to was more of the same. Janice struggled again as she tried to pull herself together. She may not have been a morning person before the apocalypse, but sleeping on the floor at work surrounded by the stifling air from 18 bodies wasn't doing me any good either.

The warm front had finally passed and cooler air hit me as I opened the front door. Most everyone was awake, the morning light shining through the glass doors and the smell of coffee wafting down the hallway. It had to be twenty degrees cooler than the day before, but that was just a guess. The bite of the air actually improved my attitude.

Another benefit of the cold air was the lack of need for the air conditioner. Dr. Kramer took me outside and showed me his generator backup system. He had an equipment room on the side of the building. It was part of the building with a double metal door that opened into a bank of batteries and several breaker boxes. Because one of their offices was furnished for minor surgery, a compressor and vacuum were necessary in here as well to run the equipment.

With no need for the air conditioner, the generator had not kicked on in a while. Kramer checked the propane tank gauge and was pleased that there was still 70% left. His mood improved dramatically.

"Wow," he said. "That's encouraging. We started with 85% and have only used about 15% of the propane these past four days."

"We're doing well?" I asked. I knew the answer, but his mood was so improved, I just wanted to hear a positive word or two from his mouth. We both needed it.

"I should say so," he gleamed. "We might be able to stay here for quite a bit longer. I think the electricity could last us upwards of two or three weeks."

We went back inside in a much better mental state. Breakfast was finished and bellies were full. We went back into his office and he invited me to sit with him. I suppose that I was different from everyone else there. I wasn't an employee and I wasn't a patient. Our relationship was more equitable. Not that I had anywhere near the training he had, and several of the nurses had just as much college education as me. But we spoke as equals before the power outage; and now I was the closest thing to a colleague he had.

After some light hearted discussions about Florida football, we agreed that the end of the world couldn't have come at a better time given their lack-luster performance to date. It was then that I realized I knew very little about this man.

"Dr. Kramer, I hope you don't take this wrong; but I was wondering about your family."

He stopped smiling and his demeanor softened.

I wanted to probe further, hoping I didn't open up any wounds or painful memories. I realized that I have never seen any of his family pictures. Most private offices have the obligatory picture of the wife, or wife and kids. His office was clinical and almost sterile in appearance. For all I knew, he could have been living in this room and sleeping on the couch since the day the clinic opened.

"I expect that they are doing rather well." He finally said. "They have a backup generator like we do here and they are surrounded by enough land that I would expect that they will ride this out just fine."

"That's good to hear," I replied. "I just realized that I've never spoken with you about them. I guess it's because I've never seen any pictures here in your office."

"True," he replied. "I don't keep any here."

"You know," I said, "that's rather unusual. I've been in many offices and I think you're the only one I know that doesn't have at least one picture of someone on the desk or wall."

"It's a conscious decision, Charlie." He replied. "I like to separate my life into work and family. When I am at work, I work. When I am at home, I put my attention into them. I don't like to mix the two."

"I suppose I can understand that," I said. "But don't you find comfort in seeing someone's picture while you are here dealing with the stress of the job?"

"No, it just reminds me that I have a better place where I could be. It's a distraction that might take my concentration away from my job and my patients."

He pointed over my shoulder at a ceiling-to-wall bookshelf filled with medical periodicals.

"I have to read all of those journals," he stated. "They come every month, over a dozen scientific periodicals. It consumes me while I'm here. I don't want to miss reading an article that might just save someone's life because I was distracted by my wife's beautiful smile or my children's happy faces. I can't take that chance."

I understood now. I understood that he was one of the few people I've met that allows for no wasted time. There was no downtime for Dr. Kramer, whether it was at work or at home.

Before I could say more, he continued with the conversation.

"We bought some land out west of here," he said. "My wife and I both love the country. I was raised on a small farm in West Virginia and decided to head south to leave the country behind. Truth be told, I hated the snow.

But after college in Gainesville, I began to realize that I still loved the country-life. My last residency in Cleveland cinched it for me. The snow and cold were brutal, and working in a larger city just didn't sit well with me."

"Well, you sure didn't pick a quiet spot here in Orlando," I countered.

"No," he smirked back. "I didn't figure on all the growth. When I got here in 1985, the city was still manageable. More importantly, my lovely wife is from the area; and with kids and a desire to avoid the snow, we agreed on Orlando. But, only if we could get out into the country and have a tract of land."

"So here you are," I chided him.

"Yes," he happily sighed. "Here I am."

"How far away is your house?"

"Not far from Monteverde," he replied. "About 20 miles away."

There was a knock on the door as our friendly conversation was interrupted. Peg stuck her head in and informed us that several of the patients and staff wanted to have a meeting.

We followed her out to the waiting room where all had assembled. One of the patients began the conversation.

"Dr. Kramer," he started. "First I want to thank you for giving us shelter these past few days. But my wife and I feel that we need to start back home now that the weather has cooled off a bit."

The man, in his late 60s, received several nods from like-minded people, including several of the staff.

"Well, certainly." He replied. "But how far do you have to travel?"

Several patients began to speak at once. When it was all said and done, six of the eleven patients and the remaining staff members except for Peg and Janice had decided to return home.

"We need some food and water to make the trip," the patient continued. "We were wondering if you could help us with that."

Dr. Kramer had them all write down where they had to travel and they determined how much food they would need. We collected several pillowcases from laundry and created sacks that they could use to transport their food and personal items.

By noon, all that wanted to leave had left, most living within ten miles of the facility. The drop in temperature would help them get home. More importantly, the rapid loss of civility meant that the longer they waited, the more dangerous it would become.

After they departed, we took inventory of our remaining supplies. We needed more. That meant another trip to Publix. But with the sounds coming from down the street, it looked like Publix's official advertising motto, "*Where Shopping is a Pleasure*," might not bear out.

Dr. Kramer stood on the front stoop of the building, looking down toward the grocery store, growing more concerned as groups of people were walking and trotting down the road towards what was sounding more and more like a riot in the making.

"We need to go now," Dr. Kramer said. "And I need to go with you."

Janice, Dr. Kramer and I went back into the office and informed the remaining patients that we were going on a shopping trip. The remaining five patients were almost too old to walk to their cars, let alone strong enough to walk two long blocks. Dr. Kramer left Peg in charge, making sure they locked the doors.

Before we left, he took Janice and me into the break room. He opened a drawer, and digging deep behind the plastic utensil tray, he pulled out two large steak knives, handing one to each of us.

"Take these!" He said as he handed one knife to each of us. Each knife still had its cardboard protector covering the edge and tip.

"I can't use this!" Janice stated.

"Take it," he stated again. "You may be glad you have it."

"Do you really think we'll need this," I stated. "Just to go to the grocery store?"

"It's no longer a store," he replied. "It's a war zone."

And with that, he spun on his heels and marched out the front. I heard Peg lock the door behind us, an unmistakable click that could be heard above the growing din coming from down the street. Janice looked at me and shivered. She buttoned up her lab coat all the way to the top. It wasn't nearly cold enough to need to do that, but I felt the same sense of vulnerability and buttoned my coat as well. Had it not been for Dr. Kramer's unwavering strides, I might never have been able to begin our journey. But seeing him walking with a purpose towards the gathering mob, put some spine in me; and we quickly caught up with him.

I placed my hand in my lab coat pocket and fondled the handle of the knife. As if he had some extra-sensory perception, Dr. Kramer craned his neck towards us.

"Don't forget to take the sheath off the knife if you need it," he said.

Fortunately, our visit went without a hitch but I just knew things were moving quickly in a bad direction.

CHAPTER 14

Day 5

Charlie

Publix Grocery Store, Kirkman Road

A couple more days went by and Dr. Kramer strode down the sidewalk and stopped short of the shopping plaza parking lot. Hundreds of people were clustered around the front entrance to the grocery store. The doors had been closed and metal storm shutters covered the windows while a retractable metal gate was in place over the front door. People were pounding on the metal gate, demanding to be let in.

We tentatively worked our way to the side of the building, standing next to the windows by the front entrance. The storm shutters covered all of the window except for the very outside edge. We were standing there, trying to decide what to do next, when I heard a tapping from the inside of the store. Someone was rapping their keys or some other metal object on the window from the inside.

I pressed my face against the window and peered into the dark slit where the shutter failed to cover the edge of the glass. Suddenly, a flashlight shone from within, illuminating someone's face in front of me. It was the boy that Janice had talked into letting us into the store. He backed up from the window a bit and I could see him shining his flashlight on his hand. It was pointing back to the right where we had gone the last time to get in the back door.

I grabbed Janice and she peered into the window as well, confirming the boy's intention to let us in the back once again. Janice told Dr. Kramer what had just happened and we proceeded around back where we found the young man waiting. Janice roughed up his hair as we walked passed him and into the darkened store.

"Hi, my name is Garrett," he said as he closed the door. We could see a battery-powered lantern sitting in the front of the store. Garrett led us to the lighted spot where Mr. Wayneright and two other employees were seated.

"Hello, Dan." Dr. Kramer said to the store manager.

"Dr. Kramer," he replied. "I wish I could give you a better welcome." They shook hands warmly.

"How's you dad doing?" the doctor asked.

"Alive!" the manager replied. "Thanks to you."

"It was nothing," he responded to the compliment. They both knew that was a lie.

"Doc!" Mr. Wayneright said. "I hope you can tell me what the hell is going on."

"Let's go to your office, so we can talk a bit," he replied.

Dr. Kramer turned to Janice and me and pointed to the aisles of food behind us.

"You two ladies," he commanded. "Get your list and see if your friend can help you gather what we need."

Janice hooked her arm around Garrett's and we stalked off to gather what we could.

"What's going on?" Garrett asked after we left the other two. "Why is this happening?"

I glanced at Janice and she gave me a nod. So I explained, the best I could, what Dr. Kramer had told me.

After we had gathered about half of what we needed, I had finished telling him what was causing the power loss and what we had done the last three days.

"Wow," he sighed. "And I thought we had it bad."

"What about you," I asked. "Where do you live?"

"I'm a student at Valencia State College," he replied. "Been working here while I take classes. My apartment is only about a mile from here, but my family lives near Ocala."

"Why here? I mean, why not another state College near you?"

"Computers," he replied. He reached onto one of the shelves and shoveled a dozen cans of spam into our cart. "I want to get a computer degree from U.C.F., and I am guaranteed entry if I finish my second year here at Valencia."

U.C.F. had a premier computer department. Their ties with the military in computer simulation were known throughout the country with multiple startup simulator companies springing up in the metro Orlando area. It was very difficult department to get in, but Garrett had found a backdoor to the competitive program. Very smart.

We finished our list and made our way back to the other two employees that had stayed with the store. We spent the next few minutes waiting for the doctor, learning that the others simply lived too far to make the walk. Both were over 60 years old and decided they couldn't make the journey. All were afraid of what was happening and both were desperate to get home.

Just then, Mr. Wayneright and Dr. Kramer returned from the manager's office.

"Garrett, Carla and Ed," he started. "I want you to make up four carts with these items and take them to the loading dock." He handed a list to the three employees. Their questioning looks prompted him to continue his instructions.

"If Dr. Kramer is correct, and I have never had cause to doubt him," he stated. "We're not going to have control of the situation for much longer. Apparently, an EMP has taken out all electronics…"

Mr. Wayneright droned on to the three people, repeating Dr. Kramer's theory. Janice and I tuned it all out, having heard it all before and uncomfortable with the thought that he was correct. Nothing like bad news repeated to shut a brain down.

When he was finished, Dr. Kramer excused us and we left out the back once again.

"What are they going to do?" I asked.

"They're making up their own survival package. He's going to stash it all in one of the dumpsters out back when they need to abandon the store. I just hope they have the time to clear out before it gets too violent."

Suddenly, Janice stopped.

"I'll be right back," she said. "Give me a minute."

She sprinted back to the lighted area where the Publix employees were gathered. After a minute or so, she returned and we left the building pushing our cart down the long backside of the plaza, out the rear delivery entrance and onto Kirkman road about two hundred yards from the grocery store's front door. Not an hour had passed since we first arrived and the mob that was waiting to get fed was easily double the size. At least five hundred people were pressed against the metal shutters. A steady hammering of fists was starting to come from the ones in front as they screamed, demanding to be let in.

"Why did you go back into the store when we were leaving?" I asked Janice.

"I told Garrett to come find us when it hits the fan," she said.

At first, I thought she was playing games with the poor kid. But the look in her eyes told me otherwise. There was real concern in them, and as she looked passed me to the growing crowd, I could tell it was only going to get worse.

CHAPTER 15

Day 5-6

Charlie

Kirkman Specialty Clinic

Evening had come, and the sound of gunfire had begun in earnest. We kept the lights off, for fear of giving away our location, and that there was power to the building. Dr. Kramer had created piles of food and medicine, one for each of the remaining patients as well one for himself. Janice and I were set with our backpacks that were nicely tucked in the closet.

"Charlie," he said. "My office, please."

I followed him back, the way lit by a small flashlight he produced from his pocket. We sat in the break room and he grabbed a couple of Cokes from the refrigerator. We popped them and each took a sip.

"At some point," he said. "You two need to leave. It's dangerous, and only going to get more so over the next week. And before you say anything," he continued. "Realize that by next week, two women walking with supplies won't last a day out there. You'll be dead, or worse, when people get truly hungry."

"Doc," I replied. "I can't. I can't leave you like this. It isn't fair."

"Never said it was. But like triage, I have to pick who is worth fighting for, and who is not. Those patients out there," he said. "They aren't going to make it. Even if I could get them home, they have no chance. Who's going to fend for them when their food runs out? The best I can hope for is that they can spend their last days with family or friends."

"But you two," he continued. "You two do have a chance and you need to take it now."

Just then, we heard something that we hadn't heard in days. The sound of a truck, and by the deep growling of its engine and pitch of the noise, it sounded like something big.

We both sprinted to the front door and out onto Kirkman road. Looking down the six-lane street, we could see a dump truck rumbling up from the interstate, knocking aside any stalled car that happened to get in the way. From the sound of the giant beast, and the rough way the gears were being shifted, it seemed that the driver didn't have too much time behind its wheel.

"I thought you said nothing was working." I said. "Does this mean it's over?"

Dr. Kramer said nothing, but continued to stare at the truck as it turned into the grocery store parking lot and aimed itself directly at the front door. The horror of what was coming mesmerized me and kept me from turning away as it smashed through dozens of people that simply didn't move fast enough to get out of the way. Bodies were flattened, crushed or dismembered as it plowed into the front of the store and blasted a hole in the building.

The hundreds of the remaining uninjured people flooded through the breach, trampling the already fallen and smashing those that were too slow. Janice screamed and dropped to her knees as I finally turned away from a sight I knew would haunt me for many nights to come.

I joined Janice, squatting next to her, holding her as she sobbed. The terror and uncertainty of the past few days finally bursting forth through her tears and wails. Just what had people become in a few short days?

"Come on girls," he said. "Back in the building."

"We have to…" Janice choked. "We have to ggggo and help."

"No," Dr. Kramer gently replied. "No we don't. There is nothing you can do for any of them now. They are all too far gone. Only more death waits for you down there."

He guided us back to the office where we told the others what we had seen. I followed Dr. Kramer back to the break room and confronted him.

He told me that vehicles wouldn't work, and I just witnessed a dump truck smash over a dozen people to death.

"I though you said nothing was working!" I shouted.

"Nothing with computers," he calmly replied. "A lot of heavy equipment and older cars have a good chance of being in working order since they don't rely on computers to run. But just about any car less than 30 years old is out for the count."

I briefly stared as his dark silhouette, then went back to the waiting room where Janice sat in the corner, a blanket wrapped around her as she scrunched up in one of the reception room chairs. Her sobbing had subsided, but she didn't respond when I sat down next to her. I couldn't see much in the dark, but I could tell she was almost in shock. Her breathing was quick and shallow, and I could feel her tremble as I gently checked her pulse. It was rapid and her skin was a bit clammy. I got Dr. Kramer, who guided her back to the first surgical suite and laid her down on the padded table. I got some additional blankets to make a pillow. I retrieved a chair from the reception area and sat next to her, holding her hand under the covers, whispering that everything was going to turn out just fine.

After a while, I must have dozed off. I was jolted to my feet, when more gunfire erupted outside. This time, however, it was close! I jumped up, my neck sore from leaning against the back of the chair, and quickly moved to the reception area. Dr. Kramer was already there, standing in the front door staring down the street toward the Publix. I was shocked as I heard the sound of several cars racing about the parking lot down the street. Several old sedans were chasing down stragglers as they sprinted out of the grocery store. Suddenly, gunfire erupted from the back window of a large four door Chevy, and two looters dropped to the ground, shot as they ran. A total of three old vehicles circled the pavement, like an old-style wagon train spinning about, only this circle spat death at anyone who exited the store. Whooping came from the attackers and cries from the victims as everyone in the store scattered to the wind, hoping to avoid the gunfire.

We watched as the cars finally stopped in front of the Publix, and almost a dozen men dashed into the store, illuminated by the high beam headlights from the cars. More gunfire exploded and after a minute or two, things settled down. Suddenly, another flurry of gunshots bellowed forth from the store and all went quiet. We peered down the road and watched as food and other items were brought out and piled into the cars' massive trunks. A half an hour went by before two of the cars turned back and went south, away from our clinic.

The third car remained, its lights beaming into the hole left by the dump truck earlier that day. After a few more minutes, we could see the three remaining men loading prescription bottles into the back seat of the car.

"Druggies," Dr. Kramer said. "We better get inside now."

We shut the glass front door and he locked it.

"Everyone," he said. "Get to the back of the building. I need you to clear the reception room."

We all made our way to the back, where all were deposited in the last of four surgical rooms. As Dr. Kramer and I went back to the reception area, he told me of his concerns that the looters would find this office and come looking for drugs.

We moved enough waiting room chairs to the back to handle all the remaining patients. I made my way into the first surgery room to be with Janice as she shakily came out of her stupor. I filled her in on what was happening, when we heard the sound of a car speed into our parking lot and abruptly stop, its headlights shining into the waiting room.

"Quick!" Dr. Kramer hissed. "Find a place to hide, and for God's sake, get out your knife!"

I reached into my pocket and felt the cardboard cover, slipping it off after removing the knife from my jacket. My hands trembled as I pressed against Janice. We cowered in the corner of the room, trying to hide behind a crash cart. It wouldn't do us much good if the druggies had a flashlight.

Dr. Kramer shut the door as he left the room and we both smashed our bodies together, two shivering girls getting ready to face people that had just run over, shot or beat to death any number of folks. Just to get a pill. Just to stay high. Civilization was falling around us. I was not prepared.

A minute passed, when we heard the crash of broken glass. A moment later, the front door clicked open. The looters must have reached through the smashed door and twisted open the dead bolt. They were in! I could hear them as they excitedly talked, doors being kicked open as they marched down the hall. Tables were being overturned and chairs and Lord knows what else were being thrown against the walls. More shattered glass when the break room right next door was feeling the brunt of the lunatics as they moved inexorably towards our room. Janice muffled a cry as the refrigerator was slammed to the ground in the next room. I held her with my left arm, my right arm holding the pitifully small knife. I had decided that I was not going to be taken without a fight. *Damn them,* I thought. *I will die before I'd let them take me, or Janice, or the patients.* I knew death was waiting, but at least, I had a chance if I stuck. I wasn't going to let the bastards get me without a price. Anyway, that is what I told myself.

I steeled myself for what I knew was coming next. The sounds from the break room had stopped, and I could see a beam of light shining under our surgical room door as the punk stepped in front of our hiding place. I let go of Janice, and braced myself. I would lunge at the son of a bitch, and stick him before he could get us. My legs were taut, as I envisioned myself in the starting blocks one of the hundreds of swim meets I had participated in. I was coiled and ready when the door exploded inward, a heavy kick from the scumbag sending it off its hinges and flying into the room.

That, I wasn't prepared for. The violence of his entrance, and the door crashing back at me held me momentarily stunned. By the time I recovered, the brute was shining his flashlight directly at Janice and me, freezing us in place. The vision of a deer in the headlights suddenly became reality as my muscles refused to budge. There we were, squatting behind a mobile crash cart, me holding a pitiful knife, and no doubt, the druggie holding a gun. We were screwed.

"Hey Darrell," the punk screamed over his shoulder. "Lookie what I found here!"

I couldn't see at all, the flashlight blinding me, keeping me from even attempting to fight back. I had no idea where he was other than somewhere behind the intense white beam. As I started to stand up, the druggie hissed back.

"Drop that knife, or I'll shoot you and yer friend dead! Drop it now!"

I held on, trying to find a way to strike back. We were trapped, and there was no way out. I lost all hope, and dropped the knife to the tile floor where it bounced with a crisp ring against the ceramic tile.

"Awww," he said. "Now that's a good girl. I ain't gonna kill ya. Just look at you two, pretty as all get out. Naw, we ain't gonna kill something as pretty as you! We just came to get us some party pills, and here we found us some party girls!"

The thug yelled back for his companions. "Hey Darrell! In here! I done found some…"

Suddenly the flashlight toppled out of his hand and onto the floor at his feet. I heard a sudden gasp. The brute stumbled into the room and went down hard on the tile floor, the flashlight illuminating his upper body. A second person crashed on top of him and Janice and I leapt back to the wall. When the flashlight had finally settled down, I saw Dr. Kramer straddling the man's back, an I.V. pole in the back of the thug's head and sticking out of his mouth on the other side.

"Are you girls alright?" He asked.

I was too stunned for words. I just saw Dr. Kramer jam a stainless steel rod through a man's head. He had just saved our lives.

"Where is his gun?" He quickly asked.

"I… I don't know" I stuttered.

Dr. Kramer grabbed the flashlight out of the rapidly pooling blood on the floor and began to search the surgical room's floor for the man's gun.

"I don't see it!" he cried. "It has got to be here somewhere!"

It only took a few seconds to search the small room. There was no gun!

Just then, another flashlight shone at us from the doorway. A second hood had arrived and the sound of a gun's hammer cocking back left no doubt about who had a firearm.

"Damn you!" he shouted, looking at his fallen friend. "You son of a bitches! Ya killed him. Now, Git against the wall… NOW!"

The three of us raised our hands and backed up until we could move no more. Once again, the flashlight blinded us as the thug moved forward to his fallen companion.

"Look what you've done! I'm gonna shoot all three of you, you bastards! I should make you suffer!"

I waited for the first bullet to come. I closed my eyes. I didn't want to see it coming. For all my bravado earlier, I felt so hopeless and alone, I just wanted it to end. I wasn't ready to die, but I knew deep in my heart that it was my time. All I could do was think about my mom and dad and pray that I wasn't going to suffer.

A loud thud broke the silence of the room, and the second man's flashlight fell to the floor. A second thump woke me from my death trance and I could see the flashlight shining on the man where he was now laying on the floor next to his friend, blood dripping down the side of his face onto the floor. His body twitched once and became still. Quickly, someone grabbed the fallen man's light and I heard a voice like an angel.

"Hey guys," the mystery man said. "Are you alright?"

"Yeah!" I said shakily.

Then I quickly followed up. "Who are you!?"

"Oh! Sorry,"

With that, our savior shone the light back on himself. He carried a tire jack and wore a Publix uniform.

"It's me, Garrett!" He said. "Janice invited me to join the party. I hope that's OK!"

"Garrett! Thank God!" Dr. Kramer shouted. "There's at least one more out there!"

Dr. Kramer shone the flashlight on the floor and found the second man's revolver lying next to his body. He scooped it and hustled out into the hallway, pointing the gun down toward the lobby and front door.

"It's O.K." Garrett said, stopping Dr. Kramer. "There was one more. He's by the car. But he's dead, too."

"I had two tire irons" he continued. "The other one's out there. I crushed the guy's skull while he was smoking. Just couldn't bring myself to pull the crowbar back out of his head."

Garrett began to shake, his flashlight beam bouncing around the room as his body dumped the adrenalin that comes from a fight or flight situation. Dr. Kramer put his arm around the young man and gently took his flashlight.

"Come   on, son." The doctor whispered. "You saved our lives. Let's find a chair while I go outside and clean up the mess."

The four of us returned to the waiting room where we sat Garrett down. Janice retrieved a Coke from the tumbled refrigerator and sat next to him, brushing his hair and holding his hand. Thank goodness she bonded with this guy. It saved us all. I had no doubt that the patients and the doctor would have been killed, and Janice and I would be in whatever hell-hole those creeps inhabited. Rape would have been the best we could have hoped for. It was unimaginable.

A few minutes later, the doctor had gathered the patients and we all sat in the reception area. Dr. Kramer found the first man's pistol in the hallway by the room Janice and I had hidden in. There was a third gun in the car. Dr. Kramer turned the old vehicle off and returned to the office. We let Garrett calm down a bit then heard about the horrors down at Publix.

It seems that the dump truck had blasted its way through the front entrance, taking out the other two employees. Carla and Ed were crushed where they were preparing to open the doors and feed the crowd outside. Mr. Wayneright and Garrett were in the back gathering more food when the wall exploded in and the truck crushed his poor co-workers. They quickly took refuge in the manager's office and locked the metal door, unable to prevent the looting. There was nothing they could do. The mob was too large and too desperate. Their need too great.

After hours of watching the carnage through the upstairs glass window, the crowd began to settle down. Most had loaded up what they could and retreated back to where they came from. Mr. Wayneright decided it was time to abandon ship and he and Garrett proceeded down to the main level. They needed to get out of there, go to their stash in the dumpster behind the building, and make their way out of the area. For Garrett, that meant finding Janice. For his manager, it meant a long walk to his home in Kissimmee.

When they reached the main floor, the gunfire began. Looters were caught in the middle. Some ran out into the melee, while others fled to the back of the store, seeking cover from the fusillade of bullets. The two retreated once again and watched as almost a dozen thugs entered the store and looted what was left. A number of people were trapped as the back entrance had been locked shut. Mr. Wayneright still held the key.

Trapped between the back of the store and the open front door, they begged and pleaded to be let go. The thugs began to shoot them one at a time. Mr. Wayneright couldn't take it anymore. He left Garrett in the upstairs manager's office, leaving his keychain with the young man but removing the pharmacy cage key, and hurried down to try and bargain with the druggies. They were rattling the metal cage that had been locked down to the floor, trying to get to the narcotics in the back.

Garrett watched as Mr. Wayneright flagged down the criminals. The gunfire abated while they talked. They made their way to the pharmacy and the cage was unlocked, giving the hooligans everything they wanted. Mr. Wayneright turned to face the remaining trapped people and pointed them to the front opening. It seemed that he had negotiated their safe passage by opening the pharmacy gates. That is, until one of them pointed his pistol at the back of the kind manager's head and pulled the trigger. Before his body hit the floor, the remaining six people were shot as well as almost a dozen guns opened fire on the unarmed group. It was over in seconds.

"I couldn't believe it!" Garrett said. "He did everything he could to protect those people, but it didn't matter. He gave them everything they wanted but they shot him like a dog."

"Lesson learned." Dr. Kramer finally said. "There is no room for trust outside of this group. Trust needs to be hard won and certain before it is given. I want all of you to remember this!"

"Well," Garrett concluded. "After they looted everything and left the building, I went out toward the front of the store and heard them talking outside about your office. They wanted more drugs. So I got a couple of crowbars from the docking area and got here as fast as I could. There were only three of them and by the time I got up here, two were in the building and one stood by the car smoking a cigarette. He never heard me come up behind him. After seeing Mr. Wayneright killed by those sickos, it was terribly easy to smash the punk's head. I just wanted to make them pay for what they did. And I couldn't let anything happen to you guys."

We sat in silence, considering what had just happened. Dr. Kramer, as usual, was the first to act. He stood up and faced us.

"Well," he started. "Out of tragedy comes opportunity. We now have a functional car and supplies in the dumpster."

"It will be light in an hour or two." He continued. "Charlie, you and I will go down to the dumpster after I inventory the stolen items in the car and retrieve the supplies. Then, we can get the hell out of here."

Nothing ever had sounded so good to my ears.

CHAPTER 16

Day 6

John Drosky

South Orlando

Officer Drosky sat on the front porch of the one story house. After finding the two bodies in the back bedroom, he spent the next few days helping those in the neighborhood cope with the new realities they faced. It was frustrating to watch civilization rapidly disappear. The two local gas and go shops were a total loss, having been broken into and vandalized the third night he slept.

After the second night in the house, the smell from the back bedroom forced him to duct tape the door's seams. His food supplies, at least the ones that he wasn't using in his emergency kit, were rapidly drawing to an end and John felt he had done all he could with the limited resources he had at his disposal. He was throwing buckets of water on a forest fire. It was futile to do much more. It was time to make his way back to headquarters and check in with his superiors.

The morning air was crisp and cold when John went back inside and gathered his backpack and supplies. He wore his civilian clothes, his police uniform stuffed in the backpack with the other items he was to carry. His "Batman" duty belt was on his waist with his Sig 226 holstered and a couple of spare magazines. He manufactured a sling for his shotgun and it hung from his right shoulder. His patrol car still sat in front of the house as he closed the front door to the dead couple's home he had occupied the past five days. He had completed a final, quick check for anything of value in both the house and his vehicle earlier so he began the walk downtown. *It shouldn't take too long,* he thought to himself. *It's less than three miles.*

He strode north to Colonial drive and gazed right down the six lane road. Smoke still rose from the Executive airport where a jumbo jet had tried to land. The pilot attempted to use the short runway to glide his beast to the ground, but in the end, there was too little real estate and too much mass to stop. It slammed into one of the numerous hangers that lined the runway and burst into flames. With no firetrucks or power, the wreckage created a series of smaller fuel fires that spread from hanger to hanger, and plane to plane. By the third day, most of the buildings had been reduced to ashes. The only thing John could see as he started down the road was the Southwest emblem on the tail of the doomed jetliner. It was the only part of the jet to survive the inferno.

The walk to the station was remarkably serene. John always liked early starts, and with the sunrise at his back as he made his way west towards downtown, it gave the city a lightness that belied the reality of the situation. As he approached the downtown area and its blocks of high rise office buildings and condominiums, vandalism was starting to show itself. Every store that could have held something of value had been broken into and ransacked. Another gas station at the corner of Orange and Colonial was gutted and burned. A pharmacy and local sandwich shop also suffered similar fates.

Checking down one small side street, John saw a body on the grass of a renovated home. The early 1900's brick mansion had been converted into an attorney's office. The lawn was littered with trash and as John hustled down the street to check the victim, he quickly realized she was beyond help. Her clothing ripped from her body, a knife buried in her chest, the poor woman had been sexually brutalized and killed where she laid. John made his way up to her body. He moved her lifeless form to the flower bed next to the broken out front door of the mansion. John retrieved his sidearm and entered the house. Once he was inside and confirmed a lack of occupants, he brought the body into the old house and laid her on a couch in a reception room to the right of the front entrance. He covered her form with a blanket from a closet in the hallway. After finding no identification, he said a quick prayer and went back on his way.

A few minutes later, John crossed under Interstate 4 and turned left onto Hughey Street and gazed down the road to the OPD headquarters.

"My God!" He said to himself. He stared at dozens of vehicles a quarter mile away, many moving about. Mostly large yellow school busses and HUMVEEs. Even a few modern MRAPS. They were clustered in front of the old headquarter building, parked end to end under the I-4 overpass parking spaces that sat across from headquarters. Several busses idled on the street, their accordion doors open and engines spewing diesel smoke into the air. All at once, civilization seemed not so far away. It was with a lighter step that John rapidly walked to the front of the building to present his credentials to a guard that stood watch.

Before he could reach the stairs to the front door, two DHS agents in full military gear appeared from behind one of the idling busses and brought their M4 rifles to bare on the policeman.

"HALT!" One man cried. "DROP YOUR WEAPONS NOW!"

John forgot he was in civilian clothing and quickly dropped to his knees. He unslung the shotgun from his shoulder and laid it on the ground. He raised both hands high in the air and replied.

"John Drosky, OPD, reporting for duty!" he shouted.

The DHS agents were in black military gear. A "POLICE" Morale patch was stuck to his Velcro Identifier on the front of their plate carriers. They were in full kit, with Kevlar helmet, a battle belt with full load out of 556 ammunition. A side arm with two spare magazines rounded out the firepower. On their shoulders were the DHS patch he had learned to recognize over the years of federal and local interaction. John didn't move a muscle.

Both agents approached Drosky and covered him. They eventually took his shotgun and pistol from his holster. They finally frisked him and zip tied his hands behind his back.

"We'll have to check this out," one of them said. "Stay seated while we verify your identification."

One of them, the older of the two, went into the building with John's identification while the other stood guard. The younger one, younger than John by his looks, bounced back and forth on his heels as he stood guard over his prisoner.

"Don't worry," the young agent said. "We just need to make sure you are who you say you are."

"No big deal," John replied. "I get it. I could have capped John Drosky and taken his weapons and I.D. No problem."

The agent seemed to relax a bit, his rocking motion steadied. But John noted that he wasn't well trained. For starters, the young man failed to keep an eye on his surroundings while his partner was in the building. In an amateurish sort of way, it felt like the kid was playing soldier and not well versed at his job. He glanced at a few woman that passed by, trying to strike up a conversation with one attractive girl. As the minutes passed, he even stopped watching John and fumbled in his pocket for some dip. Retrieving a can of Skoal, he actually put his rifle butt down on the ground, leaning it against his legs so he could use both hands to place the cut tobacco between his cheek and gums. He actually had the barrel of his firearm pointing up at his body, effectively putting his head in the line of fire. Instructors called that "lasing" as if you were pointing a laser at someone or something not meant to be pointed at with your rifle. It was inexcusable, but given the state of things, John chalked it up to desperation and situation. You take what is available and use it to the best of your abilities. DHS was using the assets they could.

John took pity on the kid and got his attention.

"Hey… kid!" he said in a low voice.

The young man turned to look at John who still sat on the sidewalk.

"No one gave you permission to talk!" He stammered back, the military rifle still butt down on the ground, its barrel pointing up at his chin as it leaned on his leg.

"No offense, but you need to be more careful where you point your rifle."

"What the hell are you talking about? I can point it wherever I want."

"I mean," John softly replied in his most gentle and non-threatening tone. "Don't let your C.O. see you with your rifle like that. You're lasing yourself."

"What do you mean?" The kid asked. John's 'concerned parent' voice, the one he used to diffuse situations on the street, seemed to disarm the young man.

"You know," John replied. "Lasing. Pointing the barrel at something you don't want to kill or break."

The kid gave him a perplexed look, so John continued. *My God,* John thought, *how deep in the hole did DHS have to go to get this kid?*

"You know," John replied. "In your firearm training. Never point the barrel of the gun at friends. It's one of the four rules of firearm safety."

The kid still looked lost, so John finally laid it out for him.

"Kid," he stated in his 'stern father' voice. "Look down at your rifle. Where the hell is the barrel pointing?"

The young DHS agent looked down at his firearm and stared directly into the loaded chamber of his own battle rifle.

"HOLY SHIT!" he cried and brought the firearm back to his 'low ready' position. Barrel pointing slightly down and slightly away from John.

"That's what I'm talking about," John said in his 'concerned' voice. "I just didn't want anything to happen to you."

The young man was momentarily embarrassed, a red flush rising in his cheeks. *Cripes,* John thought, *is this kid cherry or what?*

"Don't worry about it, kid. This world is upside down. It's easy to lose track of your training when all hell breaks loose. In a bit, it'll come back. Always does as long as your sergeants keep track of you."

The young man shuffled his feet, failing to make eye contact with John. It was an awkward moment that seemed to last for minutes. In reality, some few seconds later, another bus pulled in front of the building, disgorging a number workers and DHS agents.

"John?" Drosky heard from the sidewalk to his right. John looked over and saw one of the OPD dispatchers where she had stopped on the walkway. Tanya Culverson was known for her cool demeanor under pressure. All the officers recognized her when her voice came over the radio. She rarely sent the police into a situation without thoroughly wringing every last bit of information from the caller. It was a difficult and delicate job. She needed to balance the urgency of the call with the need for vital information. Information that could help the officers catch the bad guys, and most importantly, keep the OPD officers alive. John was glad she had made it.

"What the hell is going on here?" she stated to the DHS agent. "That man is OPD, and a hell of an officer. Just what's going on here?"

The young agent didn't know what to do. He was in a horrible spot with several OPD employees who were already cleared and back working in the building, standing behind Tanya lending their support.

Before things got any further out of hand, John shouted over them.

"HEY, ENOUGH! The kid's doing his job. They're following protocol."

"Well let me tell you…" Tanya shot back. "Their protocol sucks. I've been here from the beginning and they are doing things that just don't make sense. And they sure as hell aren't letting OPD make any decisions."

"I'm fine and he's doing what he is supposed to do." John replied in his 'I appreciate it' voice. "Now really. I've been out in the shit for six days. A few minutes sitting in the morning sun won't hurt me. I'll see you all inside and we can catch up."

"I'll be waiting!" Tanya shot back, giving the young man a glare that could have killed. "Look me up in transportation and relocation"

"What? Transportation and relocation of who?"

"That, Officer John Drosky, is the 64 dollar question. We'll talk, honey! Oh yeah, we are going to do a lot of talking!" And with that, the group moved on to the entrance.

"Thanks guys!" John shouted at them, receiving a wave from two of the members as they disappeared into the glass front doors.

"Thanks, man." The young agent said.

"Hey, you got a tough job here. Just stay frosty. You can't let your guard down when you're on the front line."

A few minutes later, the older agent returned and the two led John to the lobby. Multiple desks had been set up, and signs lorded over different areas. "Relocation Services," "Transportation," "Intra-agency Coordination," "Re-Education Services" and other monikers. John did a double take on the last one. *Re-education,* he said to himself. *What the hell is that?*

They led him to the chief of police's office, where a new group of employees were stationed. Gone were the old workers, replaced by DHS employees. The Chief's name was still mounted over the door, but a paper banner had been taped over it. It read: DIRECTOR OF DHS SERVICES.

They entered the room and John, hands still zip-tied behind his back, was led to one of twenty or so modules where a severe and rough-looking woman of indeterminate age stared back at him. The two agents spoke in hushed whispers to her while John stood ramrod straight, ten feet back, staring at the divider wall above the seated woman's head. She wore no uniform, but commanded the two agents to cut his tie and dismissed them from her presence like a drill sergeant crushing the spirit out of a new recruit.

She looked at the paperwork in front of her, taking her time while John maintained his stance. After a bit, she put the folder down and addressed the OPD officer.

"John Drosky," she started. "I'm surprised it took you so long to report!" Her tone of voice left no doubt that she wasn't happy with the delay in getting back after six days of absence.

"May I speak freely," John asked. He had decided that it was best to placate the new bosses. Act like the loyal Marine he once was (and always would be), and give these people some respect for responding so quickly to the emergency. The organization he saw here after only six days was next to miraculous given the federal government and its past history of cluelessness and ineffective execution of even the most basic functions. What John saw was a well-oiled emergency response. It was surprising and welcome.

"Go on," the woman simply replied.

John went on to describe his final call and the discovery of the bodies. The loss of power and his five days of trying to organize the people of the neighborhood. He concluded with his walk back and his surprise at the level of response.

"If I may say so," John concluded. "I am surprised with the federal response I've seen here. Very impressive. I hope I can help out."

The woman seemed to soften a bit with his last statement. Her eyes, ice cold the entire time, warmed slightly and she began to tap her pencil on the closed Manilla folder which held the summary of John's life. Everything from his grade school transcript (how in the heck did they get those) to his last field reports were in the paperwork. He was stunned to see such a massive amount of data on him already collected. More data that the OPD had in his personal file. It was remarkable.

"Both of my agents reported that you were co-operative and even helpful in diffusing a situation outside," she stated.

She then continued. "I see you have no political party affiliation, is that true?"

"True Ma'am."

"You don't like the politicians, Officer Drosky?" She said with a bit of sarcasm.

"I just don't pay attention to politics, Ma'am. I don't find it interesting or relevant to my day to day life." He replied, somewhat perplexed. *Why is that important?* He asked himself.

"I see that you don't own any personal firearms, is that correct?" She continued.

"No, Ma'am. My duty weapon is more than sufficient for my job." He once again replied. "And may I ask, why is that important?" John asked in his 'innocent' voice.

Her eyes flared with the questioning, but softened when she saw John's easy-going demeanor.

"Just taking inventory, Officer. Trying to keep the public safe."

John waited stoically for her to continue. She re-opened his voluminous folder and scanned several more pages. Multiple colored tabs were used to divide what looked to be an over two inch thick dossier. Finally, she closed the folder once again and addressed the OPD officer.

"I see that you were a Marine, Officer Drosky."

"We like to consider ourselves Marines for life, Ma'am. But yes, I was a Marine."

"And as a Marine, your job was?"

"To follow orders, Ma'am."

That seemed to please her. The woman set the folder aside and produced two envelopes. She set aside the dark blue envelope and gave John a white one.

"Officer Drosky, Thank you for your patience. Please go to your right, through the glass door marked intake 1. Take that hallway and follow the instructions you will find in the envelope I gave you. Go, and welcome back."

John nodded to the woman and gathered his backpack. His weapons were never returned to him, but he was sure that was going to be corrected once he was settled in.

As John walked away and around to the right, he found two doors against the far wall. The first one was marked Intake 2 and the one just passed it marked Intake 1. As he walked in front of the first door, Intake 2, he bumped into a Sheriff's deputy he had interacted with during his time on the force. He couldn't quite remember the deputy's name, but the large and surly man was grumbling under his breath as he pushed by John and went through the Intake 2 portal. John noticed that he carried a blue envelop with him. *Curious,* John thought. *There's a lot that doesn't make sense here.*

Then Officer Drosky exited through the Intake 1 door, pushing aside his doubts in the hopes of taking care of some of his more basic needs like a hot shower and a good meal. His stomach rumbled when he smelled bacon cooking somewhere down the hall. It had been a long five days and John was sure things could only get better with the level of organization he saw in front of him. Food and a hot shower! Those were his primary concerns right now… along with the over two million other souls in the Orlando metropolitan area.

CHAPTER 17

Day 6

Charlie

Kirkman Specialty Clinic

Dr. Kramer removed the two corpses, putting them with the third one on the side of the building. Janice mopped up the blood and everyone took turns in the hot shower. We were all preparing to leave and hot water might not be available for a while. The patients were given first dibs in the doctor's private lavatory. All five were elderly and seemed to take forever in the bathroom.

Dr. K ramen had decided to drive the five patients and Peg to their homes, then make his way back to his family farm in Monteverde. Janice and Garrett and I were going to walk to DeLand.

"That's a heck of a walk," Garrett said, as they loaded up the additional supplies from the dumpster into the captured Chevy.

The stash of medications had been somewhat of a surprise. Of course, the narcotics were the first thing the crooks had taken. But most pharmacies only keep a day or two of any medication on hand for sale. The drugs the punks had been searching for just aren't kept in high volume. It wasn't just for security's sake, but rather a financial decision. Just-in-time inventories had revolutionized profits in almost every industry in America. Daily deliveries kept overhead cost low and short term profits high. Unfortunately for the newly collapsed American people, that meant just a two or three day supply of food was on-hand when the lights went out. It was day six and people were already hungry.

But what pleased Dr. Kramer was the other medications he found. The criminals had actually taken all the drugs in the pharmacy, not just "the party drugs" and Dr. Kramer planned to use those to help his community. Heart and blood pressure meds were in the trunk, along with antibiotics and even prescriptions strength NSAIDs like Motrin and Aleve. The whole pharmacy was in there! Combined with Dr. Kramer's stash of samples, he would be able to help a lot of people for a very long time.

Garrett was stuck with a pillow case for a knap sack, lacking a backpack to carry his walking supplies. Janice lightheartedly needled him about looking like a little boy running away from home, with his pillow case tied to an unused I.V. pole. The poor kid (actually, we found out during our conversations that he was almost 22) was crestfallen. But Janice felt guilty after that and did her best to prop up his self-esteem with some reminders of how he had saved us all the prior evening. Young men, even the brave ones, can have an awfully fragile ego!

Dr. Kramer heard the kerfuffle about the knap sack and appeared with a pair of jeans.

"Whose jeans are those?" I asked.

"Donated," he replied and nodded toward the side staff entrance. That's where he took the bodies of the three thugs.

He got some string that he called paracord, and tied off the bottom of the pant legs, sealing them shut. He left two long loose ends on each tied off leg and then brought each of them up to the waist band and tied each end of the leg onto one of the belt loops. When he held it up, he had created a homemade backpack. The two pant legs were now shoulder straps, and the waist opening was the mouth of the pack.

"Don't worry," the doctor said. "He isn't going to need this anymore."

Garrett gave him a disgusted look.

"And yes I smelled them first. I think they're newly stolen. There's no smell to them!"

We all chuckled a little too morbidly. It was disturbing.

We loaded up what we now called the "denim backpack" with Garrett's supplies and Dr. Kramer used more para-cord to fasten together some of the belt loops from front loop to back loop, effectively sealing off most of the top. He made an "X" between four of the loops in the middle of the pack, two in the front of the pants and two in the back. He then tied the two loose ends together with a shoe tie so Garrett could easily open and close his makeshift rucksack, making it quite effective.

"Take this," Dr. Kramer said. "This is a spare belt. You can use it as a chest strap to cinch the leg straps together in the front. It'll keep the sack riding high on your back and a lot more comfortable."

Janice smirked.

"What's so funny?" Dr. Kramer asked.

Janice began to giggle, then snort as she fought to hold in her laughter. Finally, she blurted it out.

"I never thought I'd hear you worried about another man's sack riding high and comfortable!"

We all just looked at her, stunned. And as one, including Dr. Kramer, we had the best laugh I could remember in a very long time. It seemed to last forever, and was the greatest medicine I could have ever been given. All of a sudden, our situation didn't seem so bad. It was, pardon the pun, just what the doctor ordered.

Dr. Kramer brought me, Janice and Garrett into his private office while the patients gathered their belongings and took them to the car outside.

"Well," he said. "I guess this is it! I wish I could say it's been a pleasure, but I can say I am proud of the way you three handled yourselves. You were the perfect end of the world companions!"

We all giggled and got down to a more serious discussion. The doctor opened his desk drawer and withdrew the three handguns we inherited when our invaders were killed the prior evening.

"Do any of you have firearm training?" He asked.

"I do," I replied. "My dad took me to the range a number of times. But I haven't shot a gun in a few years."

He grabbed a black pistol and unloaded it by racking the slide back, ejecting the bullet in the chamber, locking it in place and ejecting the magazine. He handed me the handgun.

"It's a Hi-Point 9 mm." He stated. "It's heavy and has a stiff trigger. But it's reliable and won't let you down. It holds 8 bullets in the magazine and one in the chamber."

I hefted the firearm and disengaged the slide lock, which was the same button as the safety. Interesting. The slide snapped forward and I held the heavy handgun up in front of me, lining up this sights on the "staff only" sign attached to his bathroom door.

I grabbed the magazine and put it back in the pistol, racked the slide which put a bullet in the chamber and ejected the magazine once again. I put the previously ejected bullet back in the magazine and replaced it in the pistol.

"This will do!" I said. "It's heavy, but I like the feel of it. Like my dad used to say, more mass, less recoil."

"Well," Dr. Kramer said. "That's a great idea when you're at the range. But you have a lot of miles to cover and that gun is nearly two pounds. Can you do it?"

"I'm a Gator, Dr. Kramer!" I said, reminding him of my collegiate days. "I can do anything!"

"Oh please!" Janice shot back. "If you ever do one of those God awful Gator chomps with your arms, I promise I will snap you in half!"

"Roll Tide!" I replied with a grin.

"OK. OK. That's quite enough," the doctor said with a grin. "How about you, Janice? Do you know how to handle a firearm?"

"Sorry, Dr. Kramer. In my family, the boys did the hunting and the women did the cooking. I suppose I could use one if I had to, but I would prefer to let someone else do that."

"Suite yourself," he replied. "How about you, Garrett?"

"I can handle a pistol," he replied.

Dr. Kramer had a revolver and another black handgun on the table. Garrett picked up the black pistol and properly removed and replaced the magazine. He kept the firearm pointed away from all in the room as he manipulated the slide to gently pull it back a bit and confirm that a bullet was in the chamber.

"It's a Glock," he said.

"It's a 40 caliber," Dr. Kramer said. "It's got a 13 round magazine and I found a spare mag in the car along with two boxes of ammo, one for each pistol."

Dr. Kramer took the revolver and put it in his pocket.

"Well I've got my hunter right here!" Janice said in her sweet southern accent. Garrett smiled, turned and left the room.

"I've got one or two more things to pack," he said as he made his way to the reception room.

"I'm with him, too." Janice said and quickly followed.

"Looks like Janice found her man," Dr. Kramer said after the two had left the room.

"But he's too young," I replied. "She's almost five years older than him."

"He's a man," Dr. Kramer said in earnest. "In this new world, you'll find out soon enough that age isn't going to determine the men from the boys. Garrett killed two dangerous people for you guys, especially for Janice. Not many men out there in today's society that could or would do that."

He was right, I thought. *Just how many guys in my generation could have done what Garrett did last night? Who could you rely on in this upside down world?*

Garrett had proven himself. As I watched the two of them work together down the hall in the waiting room, I realized that they were quickly becoming a couple. I envied them. Going through the apocalypse with a partner would make things much easier. I thought I had a battle buddy in Janice, but now, I wasn't so sure. She needed protection, I wanted a partner.

Thirty minutes later, we helped the patients into the vehicle. The car was loaded with food, medical supplies and other gear that the six would use to survive the coming weeks. Dr. Kramer had a long coil of I.V tubing wrapped around his waist in the event he needed to siphon gasoline. It was both cute and sad at the same time. We hugged and kissed each other, acting like the day after Thanksgiving when all the relatives were heading home. It was a bittersweet time. We all knew that we wouldn't be seeing each other again.

Dr. Kramer handed me a paper bag just before he got into the driver's seat.

"Here, Charlie. Take these. They are for you and Janice."

I looked inside the bag and it was filled with birth control pills. I looked up and smiled.

"Gosh, Doc. I didn't know you thought of me that way!"

He chuckled and put on a serious face. "Charlie, you don't want to be pregnant out there right now. It's not going to be a place to raise a baby. Just take these and start using them if you aren't on them already. I hate to think of bearing a child in this mess."

"It's alright, doc. I don't have a boyfriend."

"Maybe not now," he replied. And in a grave whisper, he said. "And maybe you run into a situation where you didn't want to get pregnant. Or worse, a time when you didn't want to have sex."

I got his drift. My mood quickly turned serious. Getting pregnant because I wasn't careful was stupid. Getting raped may not be a choice. I shivered and Dr. Kramer grabbed me in his arms and hugged me. It was a father's hug. I needed it.

"Now!" he said to the group. "It's time to get out of here!"

He looked at the three of us and pointed down the road past the I-4 overpass. "There is a bike shop down there, and a Wal-Mart further still. But I would stay away from any store that could have food, liquor, drugs or firearms. They'll be a death trap someday, if not already. Each of you need to get a bike, however you can. By hook or crook. It will make your trip a lot quicker and maybe safer. And find a map if you can!"

With a quick wave, the good doctor jumped into the driver's seat, cranked the engine and was gone. Janice started to tear up as the big blue Chevy rumbled down to Kirkman road, made a right and shot north to begin delivering his patient's to their homes. I sighed, and as the quiet began to settle in, I realized that I felt a lot less sure of myself now that he was gone. I felt small and frail for the first time in a long while. With Dr. Kramer gone, I became very aware that I missed my family, and most of all, I missed my dad. I wanted to go home.

CHAPTER 18

Day 6

33rd Street Jail

Mike Jones was glad it was nearly over. The past five days hadn't gone well. With the power gone and over four thousand angry inmates yelling, cursing and throwing feces at him, he had just about had enough of the place. If it weren't for his brother officers, he likely would have split some inmate heads. And there had been a lot of that going on. Not the COs banging heads, but the gangs taking on each other. At least for the first three days.

They had done their best to keep the gang members separated throughout the ordeal. But with no computers available to track the prisoners' location in the complex, more often than not, competing gangs would inadvertently meet in the exercise yard or cafeteria. Almost always, blood was drawn. Things were bleak, and rumors that the food supply was dwindling didn't leave the correction officers with much hope.

Three days earlier, the warden released about 700 prisoners that were considered non-violent or within six month of release. They were drawing up a second list when miracles of miracles happened. The federal government showed up! A convoy of military vehicles pulled up to the front gates and rumor had it that they were going to be absorbing the facility into the federal government. In fact, the commander of the DHS unit had been taken to meet with the various gang leaders and within a day of his arrival and the gang violence trickled to a halt. Mike didn't know how they did it, nor did he care! But the last two days had been blissfully quiet, and the feds, or DHS or someone with some serious pull had actually brought out a working generator, allowing them to restart the muffin monster and clear the sewage from their pipes. There was even a shower available for the brass that ran hot water! And the food problem disappeared overnight. Mike had to admit it, the feds came through with flying colors.

Just then, his radio crackled to life. "Officer Mike Jones. Report to the warden's office."

Mike keyed back and replied. He would be there in ten minutes.

Mike had been sleeping in the work release center where the guards had taken over the facility. The center, designed like a dormitory, allowed for prisoners to work in the community, then return to jail at night. It provided them the chance to pull their own weight by earning an income to support their own family, pay victim restitution and reimburse the government for fees in prosecution. All these work center prisoners were low risk and had been released, freeing up space for the guards that had stayed to do their jobs. Overall, over 50% of the staff stood their ground. Mikey was proud of that. He thought it would have been a lot worse.

Mike entered the warden's office where a new group of administrators had set up shop. Several desks were present with DHS employees manning each one. Mike must have had a confused look on his face, because one of the administrators shouted out.

"Can I help you?" he yelled.

"Uh, Mike Jones reporting as requested."

"Oh yes," one of the other desk jockeys said, "right over here."

Mike took a seat in front of the man while he reviewed a thick folder in front of him.

"Oh, easy enough!" The man gushed. "You're scheduled to go to OPD headquarters where you'll be reassigned by our department there. They are processing all the Corrections Officers at their facilities."

The man took Mikes incredibly thick personnel file and placed it in a self-sealing envelope. It reminded Mike of the large white, tear resistant envelopes the post office uses for First Class Mail. The ones with the green border.

"Now you need to take this with you and report to the Orlando Police Department Headquarters building at 100 S Hughey Ave." The man continued. "There is bus service at the front gate that leaves on the hour. You have to report by midnight, tonight."

"Do I have to wait until then?" Mike asked. He was scheduled for another night shift, but that was obviously not happening if he had to report to OPD headquarters tonight.

"No, whenever you are ready," he concluded. "Anything else?" The man asked as Mike sat and tried to assimilate his new orders. Mike shook his head.

"Then go! Be off! The next bus leaves in 45 minutes and another an hour later."

Mike got up to leave but was stopped when the man handed him the envelope with his records in it. The man, a bit on the eerie side, refused to let go of the package when Mike first took hold. He tugged back hard as Mike attempted to leave.

"Under NO circumstances are you to open this package! If you do, it is a federal crime punishable by imprisonment of at least five years!"

Mike snickered, thinking the man was pulling his leg, but one look at the bureaucrat told Michael James Jones that there was no humor in his words.

"Seriously?" Michael shot back.

"Officer Jones," the man sneered back. "Don't Fuck with the DHS! Not now, nor in the immediate future. Be advised. We aren't screwing around."

Mike shook his head in amazement and lumbered off to pack his belongings and catch the next bus. It had been a strange few days. But regardless of the lack of civility of the new front office people, he was glad they were there and elated that he could leave.

He wanted to check up on his mother and two sisters, so he just had to report in tonight and find some down time to make sure the family was safe. His family lived north outside of Sanford and had a little land where his mama raised chickens, rabbits and had a nice garden. He knew that with her stores of canned and jarred food, they would be alright for now. And his mama and the sisters knew how to use a gun, having a shotgun and pistol available to protect their home. They had good neighbors too, so Mikey wasn't worried yet. Looking at the activity around him, it appeared that the corner had been turned. He would just check in, get his new assignment and take some time to see his family. *Maybe*, he thought, *I might even convince mama to put one of her older birds into a pot and cook a nice homemade chicken dinner.* That thought finally brought a grin to the big man's face. The first one in six days. It felt good to finally smile again.

About a half an hour later, Mike was found his way to the bus tagged to deliver its passengers to the OPD headquarters. With less than 4 miles of roadway to travel, it shouldn't take too long. But then again, with the stalled cars and lack of power still evident, there was no way to know how long any travel would take.

Looking down the road, Mike could see a stream of people coming off the I-4 ramp, heading away from the jail to the north. The numbers were surprising. Hundreds of people were walking along the side of the road, coming down the far ramp and continuing north on the roadway. The flow seemed endless.

"That's a lot of mouths to feed!" came a retort next to him.

Mike looked down and thought he recognized the woman standing next to him. Unsure who she was, he replied back. "Tru dat. I haven't seen that many people since the last Florida Classic Football game."

"The Cats really took it to the Rattlers, didn't they?" She replied.

The big man looked down on the little white woman and gave her a very quizzical look.

"Get back, girl!" He said with a smile. "You watched that game!"

"Every year." She replied.

"But its BCC and A&M. They're black schools. And you definitely are not black!"

"So," she replied. "I watch for the battle of the bands. And the cheerleaders! I don't care who you are! That's fun to watch."

"Huh!" Mikey snorted. *Never would have thought!* He said to himself.

"Name's Beth! Beth Ann Hildreth." She said to him and stuck out her little hand.

The big guy gently took her hand in his and replied. "Mike. Mike Jones."

"So, Mike Jones. I assume you're a corrections officer!"

"Yes ma'am. And I assume you are not!"

The little woman rang out an infectious giggle. "No sir. No I am not!"

"Didn't think so. You don't have that look."

"What look?" She deftly lobbed back. Their verbal sparring was becoming fun. "You're saying I look a little too mean for the job?"

"Well," Mike shot back, enjoying the direction of the conversation. "I didn't want to bring that up. But since you've mentioned it…"

"Watch it, buster!" She chided back. "Big guys like you have no defense for my quick, cat-like strikes! HIAAA_YAAA!" And she jumped into an exaggerated karate stance, staring up at the giggling giant next to her.

"I'm glad you recognized my superior powers, Mr. Mike. Before I was forced to use them on you. I can assure you, it would have been extremely embarrassing!"

"OK! I give up! You are the sensei!" Mike snorted at her.

"And I will call you grasshopper!" Beth replied.

"Grasshopper?" Mike genuinely asked. "Why grasshopper?"

"You know, Kung Fu. The old television show."

"Never heard of it," Mike honestly said. "Must be a white thing."

"Naw," Beth said. "More generational. I could be your mother."

"Hmmph," Mike said back.

He stared north at the walking hordes moving away from them up John Young Parkway away from the jail. He pointed at them and Beth looked where he directed.

"The way the world looks now," he said. "I don't know if I'll ever learn what you're talking about."

Beth stared up the road, watching the mass of people stagger and slog their way along the four lane street.

"Tru dat, big man!" She replied back. "Tru dat."

CHAPTER 19

Day 6

Charlie

On the Road

I strapped my book bag over my shoulders and quickly realized that jogging and CrossFit weren't the same as hiking with a load on my back. I suppose I shouldn't have been surprised at the 'revelation.' I mean, even in swimming, being a star at the 50 meter freestyle didn't translate to fame and fortune in water polo. They were two completely different events, even though they were both in the water. You would think that a medalist in the SEC championships my junior and senior year could allow me to throw a damn volleyball in the water for a full game! But when I tried once, just because it looked like fun... I lasted exactly sixteen minutes (two quarters of the four quarter match) before I gave up. These guys have to tread water, dash back and forth the length of the pool and rise up several feet like a freaking whale breaching the surface of the ocean. And they do it, non-stop, for eight-minute stints, four times in a row. I assumed they were the same muscles I used when I did my 50 and 100 meter freestyle sprints, but I quickly found out they really aren't. Water polo was a constant grind while freestyle sprinting lasted less than a minute with hours between competitions. I was a world class sprinter in swimming's version of a marathon. Now, with the prospect of having to lug 30 pounds across miles of hostile land, I was quickly being reminded of this reality. The best way to get in shape for a particular physical event or test is to practice that event. I was a jogger, wearing the minimal amount of clothing and lightest shoes when I did it. Now only an hour into our journey, I was carrying almost 30 pounds of food, clothing, water and a damn heavy handgun, and feeling it in muscles I didn't realize I had. And worse of all, we were still wandering about just south of the office looking for bicycles and hadn't started north to Janice's sister's house.

What was also taking its toll was the stress. Walking wasn't just a stroll now. We had to plan our steps, literally every step, so that we could cover each other, avoid possible traps and choke points and all the while try to stay unnoticed. The people who were out now tended to be a bit desperate. With six days of hell behind us, the desperate, stupid and criminal tended to be the boldest. I hoped we were in the first category and not the second. Of course, we had killed three men so technically we did fit the third category.

When we finally found the bicycle shop, it had been looted. I suppose it shouldn't have been a surprise with the hotels and theme parks nearby. Anyone with a home 500 miles or less from here would have been looking for any transportation to get home. Unless we wanted to take a child's pink "Barbie" bike, of which there were many left in the ransacked shop, we were now committed to our lot in life: foot refugees. At least we only had 50 or 60 miles to walk. Her sister's property was about ten miles northwest of DeLand which was about as rural as you could find in crowded Central Florida.

One big positive was our discovery of a map of the bicycle trails in Central Florida. Not having been into bicycling, I was surprised at the number and extent of the trails throughout the state. Janice and Garrett cleared a table and we laid the map down. The early morning sun was shining into the broken storefront window, giving us a nice warm light to see by. After studying the map for a bit, I realized that we could use several of these trails to pass through many parts of the city while staying off the main roads. It was becoming evident that the best way to survive was not to be seen. Another "find" was some clip on flashlights that we might find useful. But the added weight, as light as they were, made me hesitant to add the extra few ounces.

Well, I thought, *I'll be eating some food soon and that will drop the weight I'm carrying.*

We ran across an unopened five-gallon jug of water for an employee water bubbler. We swapped out the empty jug on the stand for the unopened one still in the closet and drank as much as we could before topping off our own supply. Dr. Kramer warned us to eat and drink as much as we could when the opportunity arose. It preserved our supplies.

As we scanned the map, it was apparent that most of the trails that led to just north of downtown. We were going to have to make our way through Orlando on normal paved roads before finding the bicycle trails that might hide us as we escaped the rapidly deteriorating city.

I was looking at the names of the trails when I ran across a name that echoed in my mind. The Seminole/Wekiva Trail rang a bell, and I was vaguely aware that I should know why. The southernmost trail that would help us was called Cady Way and might give us our first chance to get off the road. It began just east of downtown.

"You know," Janice said. "The neighborhoods from here to downtown aren't exactly the safest to walk."

"And that was before the shit hit the fan!" Garrett chimed in.

They were right. This damned apocalypse had really screwed up our lives. Travel now meant you couldn't just button up your car and glide past the crime and other areas that made you uncomfortable. You had to confront them.

Maybe, I thought, *that had been the problem all along. We never had to face what we weren't comfortable with. And a problem ignored will grow to a crisis unresolved.*

The more I thought about it, the less I liked the idea of going through Orlando. But when we looked at the alternatives, going around the sketchier areas of the city, we were adding days of travel. There appeared to be no alternative but to suck it up, take our chances and head straight for Orlando.

"What's going on outside?" Janice asked. "Who are all those people?"

I turned from the table and looked out onto Kirkman road. We had walked down under the I-4 overpass and found the bike shop in a strip mall about a half a mile passed the freeway onramp. Now, there was a steady stream of people walking back north toward the expressway. Not just a stream, but a flood of people. Men, women and children were marching up the road filling both north and southbound lanes, all heading north.

We grabbed a couple of maps and jogged out onto the sidewalk, watching the parade of people walk, shuffle and stumble up the road. Families and couples were dragging their luggage and children behind them like some pitiful migration across the asphalt planes of the Central Florida Serengeti.

Then, just in front of me, a woman with two small children had her rolling suitcase handle snap. A large open beach bag tumbled off the top of the rolling case spilling almost a dozen water bottles and multiple granola bars onto the pavement. It looked like she had raided the free continental breakfast bar at her hotel, and now it had all dumped out onto the road with two screaming, filthy children grabbing her torn and stained jeans. The poor woman was at her wits end and began to scramble for the lost treasure when one of the other travelers, a similarly soiled man in a tattered business suit began to steal the water and bars, shoving them into the pockets of his jacket.

"NO! THOSE ARE FOR MY CHILDREN!"

"Tough shit lady." He sniped back as he scooped up a pile of fruit and nut bars.

"Sorry buddy!" I heard and snapped my head to the left.

Garrett had his Glock out and had drawn down on the pig of a man, leveling his 40 caliber at the jerk's head. The man stopped, his eyes wide with fear. He slowly began to put the handful of bars back on the ground. I looked about and we had gotten noticed. Most stopped and retreated from Garrett and his hand cannon, but I noticed three men in the group directly behind the businessman start to move around Garrett, attempting to flank the kid. I could tell they were intrigued by the Glock in my friend's hand.

Before I could even think about it, I had my Hi-Point 9mm out and pointed at the three as they were moving off the road and around Garrett's back.

"I DON'T THINK SO!" I shouted.

They froze and immediately began to back away.

"Other side of the street, assholes. Don't fuck with us. We've killed

three already today and three more won't make a damn bit of difference…
so JUST FUCKING MOVE!"

They looked at each other and ran across the median to the other side
and disappeared into the mass of people.

I stood there, still pointing at the place where the three had just been,
my hands shaking from the rush when I felt Janice gently grasp my pistol.

"It's OK, Charlie. They're gone!" she quietly said.

I lowered my gun and turned to see a wet stain beginning to form in
the businessman's groin area. He had pissed himself. I tuned to face him
and strode up and got into his face.

"Give it all back and get the hell out of here!"

"Uh… sure!" He replied and quickly placed the stolen items back on
the pavement.

"I don't think so dipshit. Put them in her bag like a good gentleman."

He picked up the fallen items and brought them over to the woman.
The poor woman was standing in the road, her children clinging to her
legs, mouth agape. The man reloaded all the lost items into her fallen
beach bag and set it on the ground next to the mother and kids.

"Now apologize for being an asshole!" I shouted loud enough for all
to hear.

"Uh… I'm sorry." He said in a quiet voice.

"You're sorry for being an asshole! And say it loud enough for everyone
to hear!"

The man hesitated, at least until I put my hand on the butt of the
Hi-Point which had been stuffed into the front of my belt. Janice and I
both wore our scrubs, me because my business attire wasn't fit for walking
and her because she had nothing else. She wore her scrubs to work. I had
recovered my leather belt, and had that around my waist over my scrubs.
My pistol was tucked into the belt, being too heavy to be held up by the
cloth ties that kept my scrub pants up.

"Oh Come on!" He protested.

"Unless you want more than piss staining your clothes," I said. "You'll
do what I said. Now apologize for being an asshole. Otherwise, I can tell
you from experience, blood won't come out of that nice jacket of yours."

The man hesitated once more, then faced the woman.

"SORRY FOR BEING AN ASSHOLE!" He shouted.

Before I could say anything else, he sprinted across the road and disappeared into the crowd that was trying to decide if it was safe to proceed.

I turned to the woman and child, picking up the beach bag and handing it to her.

"You need to be careful," I said. "It's nasty out here and getting worse."

She smiled and thanked us, pulling the kids onto the sidewalk. We led her and her family to the parking lot of the bike store and helped her try and repair her suitcase.

While helping, we picked up some valuable information. For one, the people around us were coming from the local hotels that were accommodating the Universal studio visitors. The night before, the government had stopped by the hotels and informed them that DHS had set up processing centers to help those that were trapped. She showed me a flyer that was distributed by the federal agents with a map directing everyone to the Central Florida Fairground. People were told to take I-4 north-east toward Orlando. They were to get off on John Young Parkway, right next to the 33rd Street jail and head north. A few miles up the road, turn left and the Fairgrounds were on the right. It promised food, shelter and safety.

"Wow," I said after reading the flyer. "That's impressive!"

I showed it to Janice and Garrett. They were equally surprised at the rapid and efficient response the government had managed. I began to have some hope.

"It says, no firearms and to have some identification," Garrett said.

"What's wrong with that?" Janice asked. "You getting a little attached to your new friend?" Janice patted the top of his Glock.

"No," he replied. "I guess not. It's just that our guns have already stopped some bad shit from happening. I hate to give that up."

"You did pretty well with a tire iron, big boy!" Janice replied with a smile. "Does it say anything about tire irons?"

"No," he replied with a sheepish grin. "But I like what I have a lot more."

"Let's cross that bridge when we get to it," I said. "I vote we find this place and see what it's all about."

"I know I would appreciate it if you tagged along," the poor mother said. "I'd feel a lot safer if you were with us."

Janice picked up the younger child and nodded to me. Garrett, well, he was going where Janice went so the decision was settled.

"My name's Charlie," I said to our new walking companion.

"Theresa," she replied. "And this is Kaylee, my oldest."

"I'm five years old," the little girls said holding up all five fingers of her right hand.

"Wow," I replied. "Next year you're going to have to use two hands when you tell me your age!"

"And your friend is holding Brie, my youngest."

"I'm Janice. Hi Brie!" she said as she hoisted the little girl on her shoulder.

The young girl squealed with glee as she rode above the crowd. It was amazing how adaptable kids were, and how aware they were of the emotions around them. Her mom felt safe, so now the kids did too.

We put together another one of Dr. Kramer's make-shift Wrangler jean backpacks with one of the woman's spare pair found in the broken suitcase. We soon were loaded up, mom and her oldest child holding hands, Janice with the youngest on her shoulders and Garrett and me flanking them, hand on our pistols tucked into our front belt.

We returned to the moving mass of people and went back up the road, turned right onto the onramp and entered Interstate 4. The massive 10 lane road which starts in Daytona Beach to the Northeast cuts southwest across Central Florida and ends up in Tampa. Along the way, it crosses Orlando and takes people to Universal Studios, SeaWorld and of course, Disney World. As we got up to the elevated expressway, I could finally appreciate the immense number of people involved. Stretching for as far as I could see in both directions, thousands and thousands of people were slowly migrating east toward Orlando. That's when another wonderful tidbit of information was revealed to us.

"I guess that's what the DHS guy meant when he suggested we leave as soon as possible." The mother said. "He told us that where we were, there were about 20,000 people here in the Universal area."

"I can believe it," I said looking about us.

"Yeah, but he said there could be as many as 300,000 down by Disney. And even more from parts south. And that they were all going to be coming this way. So if we wanted to stay ahead of them, we needed to move."

I glanced back, but the crowd around me blocked my view. As we passed the numerous cars, trucks and SUVs, I ran ahead and climbed on top of a dead 18-wheeler and looked behind us to the southwest. Down the road, several miles back, a literal wall of humanity was making its way toward us. Tens of thousands of people had massed and were walking up the interstate. It was the Super Bowl and World Series multiplied by three, all moving our way.

I got down and told the rest what was happening. I sure didn't want to get caught in all that. There was no way our government could handle that mess. We all agreed that our final goal was to get to DeLand and take care of ourselves. Going to shelter and relying on the government to house hundreds of thousands of refugees along with feeding millions in such a small area was going to be impossible.

Theresa was visibly agitated at our decision, but agreed we were probably correct in our assessment. I assured her she could still change her mind when we got to the turnoff at John Young Parkway, where she only had a couple of hours walk to get to the Fairgrounds. It was with this thought in mind that we moved with a purpose up I-4 and toward the turnoff a few miles ahead. That's when our world turned upside down and death visited us once again.

CHAPTER 20

Day 6

33rd Street Jail

Mike and Beth

Mike and Beth entered the bus and took seats next to each other. So far, they were the only passengers on the large, Greyhound transport. The engine was running and door open, but no driver had yet appeared. They were scheduled to leave within the next few minutes.

"My God," Beth said. "We could have walked there by now."

"Yeah," Mike replied. "But I don't want to mix it up with all the people out there. Too much going on I don't understand."

Beth looked at Mike for several seconds, assessing the big man with renewed interest.

"So Mike," she said. "Where are you from?"

"Oh, right here in O-town." He said. "Graduated from Seminole High School."

"Did you play sports?"

"Oh sure! With my size I didn't have a choice!" he smirked. "Did alright. Nothing special. Then when I graduated I decided to be a CO."

"Why not a cop?" Beth inquired.

"Cops don't have too good a rep in my neighborhood. A CO! Now that's alright."

Beth understood. She had processed too many American black males not to get the drift that cops were the enemy in many African-American communities, even the black cops. It was a sad state and Beth didn't see any easy way out of it.

Just then, three school busses rolled into the front gate and pulled up next to the front of the Booking and Release Center. The drivers left the busses running and entered the BRC.

"That's weird," Beth said, staring at the idling behemoths.

"Probably releasing more prisoners," Mike replied. "They've been letting the short timers and non-violent go. I just don't know who else they can let out that won't be causing problems!"

They continued to watch for any sign of who was going to get the "get out of jail free" card when Mike saw a group of soldiers come out a side door or the BRC. The emergency exit went into a courtyard to the right of the main entrance to the building. It was surrounded by a ten foot chain link fence topped with razor wire.

Mike and Beth watched as eight DHS agents decked out in full kit moved into the courtyard and turned to cover another group that was a few seconds behind them.

"Hey!" Mike said. "That's Chief Braddock. And the judges!"

"You're right!" Beth replied. "Judge Bender and Hernandez."

As the two watched, the second group of people including the judges and chief moved to the wall of the building while the 8 agents kept their place about ten yards back. There were several DHS administrators talking animatedly with the captain while the two judges stood with arms crossed, listening to the conversation.

"Mike," Beth said tapping him on the shoulder. "I don't like what I'm seeing. Can you crack the window a little to see if we can hear what they're saying?"

"Sure. I was just going to do that."

Mike clasped the window clips and sliding the glass on its tracks about an inch. What the two of them heard next was forever frozen in their minds.

"I'm telling you," Captain Braddock said in a raised and angry voice, "Is that you can't do that with those thugs! I won't approve it and I promise you, I'll make sure your superiors know about it!"

"I can assure you," the head administrator said in an eerily calm and commanding voice, "that my superiors not only know about this, but have engaged me to implement these directives."

"I don't believe it!" Judge Bender shot back. "Our government can't have fallen to this level. I can promise you we will fight you tooth and nail. This is not constitutional and every corrections officer in the facility will fight you when we let them know what's going down."

The DHS administrators had moved back slightly from the other three men. Their leader, a lean and pale man, had his back to the captain and judges. He had his head down, shaking it slowly. Finally, about three paces back, he turned and with a sneer he addressed the three.

"This is a new time," he said. "This is a new world. There is no more Constitution. There are no more 'rights'. There is only power and pain. And I weld both!"

Then, without hesitation, he drew a handgun and shot Judge Bender in the head. Within another second, the eight DHS agents lit up all three men and riddled them with dozens of rounds. All three were dead before their bodies hit the dirt.

The administrator turned to scan the parking lot. Beth and Mike ducked down in time to avoid detection. After a minute, the eight agents had taken the corpses back in the building and the area was once again clear.

"Oh my God!" Beth said. "I can't believe it!"

Mike was boiling. Captain Braddock was his boss, but more importantly, he was a brother CO. Mike respected him as much as any man. There was vengeance in Mike's blood. Beth could see it when she stared up at the man-giant sitting in the seat next to her. She put her hand on Mike's shoulder.

"There's nothing we can do right now," she said quietly.

"I know," Mike said. "Ain't going to do anything stupid. But this won't stand."

"What should we do?" Beth asked. "Do we go back in or do we get out of here."

Before they could decide further, the front double doors of the BRC were flung open and several DHS agents came out, one manning each of the busses. Then, to the astonishment of both Beth and Mike, dozens

Aryan Brotherhood prisoners came out, none of which had cuffs or restraints. They joked and whooped as they spread out and entered the busses. When finally full, the three vehicles slowly turned around in the parking lot and made their way out the gate, finally turning up the ramp onto I-4.

"Jesus," Beth said. "Could that be what the Captain and judges died for?"

"Hmmph," Mike replied. "Looks like a reason to me."

Several more DHS agents came out the door, laughing and joking. Two of them went to the front gate and manned it. Beth and Mike looked at each other, having not even noticed that it was unguarded from the beginning.

"We stumbled onto an execution," Beth said.

"And they didn't want any witnesses," Mike added.

The third agent made his way toward the bus they were on. If found, the both knew they wouldn't be alive to see the sun set.

"Hide," Beth said. "Get to the back of the bus and get down."

Somehow, the two of them managed to scrunch down and avoid detection. The driver gave the back of the bus a perfunctory look and started the engine. Immediately, they felt the vehicle lurch forward, its gears ramping up as they too entered the onramp to Interstate 4. But, once on top of the interstate, instead of moving forward they came to a quick stop. The driver opened the door and hopped out, making his way behind the bus. Screams could be heard outside and both Mike and Beth risked a peek out the back window.

There, not a hundred yards behind them was a massive roadblock with MRAPs, HUMVEEs and police vehicles. All the vehicles were blocking, what looked to be the largest mass of people they had ever seen, from moving any further down the expressway. They were being pushed off the interstate and onto John Young Parkway. The problem was that a large group of people, several hundred by the looks of it, had stopped and refused to go down the ramp. It appeared that there was an impasse when out of the blue, the blockade was pulled back and the crowd that had wanted to keep using I-4 were allowed to continue their journey down the expressway.

That's when Beth spotted the Aryan Brotherhood. One of the school busses had pulled off to the side of the roadway and disgorged its passengers. With pipes and fists, the Brotherhood rushed into the crowd and began to exact a bloody revenge on the uncooperative mob that had just passed by the blockade. The DHS agents manning the roadblock simply stepped back and to the side. *Now,* both Beth and Mike thought, *things were starting to make sense.*

As the Brotherhood merged with the crowd, the two groups were indistinguishable. As far as the DHS was concerned, it was a win-win situation. Lose some uncooperative civilians, less problems for them. Lose an Aryan, no problem either. They were all sitting back, appreciating the show.

The bus driver seemed to be watching for the same reason, the sick enjoyment of observing someone else suffer. It was a modern day Coliseum with the slaughter of these innocents providing the same twisted pleasure as in ancient days. It made Beth shake. It made Mike see red.

Suddenly, a group of about 50 civilians broke from the ranks and started running up the far side of the wide concrete expressway. A whistle blew from a DHS agent at the roadblock and a second group of Aryan Brothers appeared from that area and gave pursuit. The two groups were destined to meet, and by both Mike and Beth's estimation, they were going to collide right at their location.

The bus driver must have figured out the same thing, because he turned and strode back to the bus. Mike moved up and hid about five rows from the front. The driver entered the bus and shut the door, locking it in place. He removed his sidearm and stood at the door of the bus and watched out the front window where the two groups had finally met. There were about a dozen thugs from the white gang and they laid into the unarmed group of civilians the way a pack of wolves would attack a flock of sheep. As he stood, staring out the front glass, the last thing the driver would ever remember was the feeling of surprise when saw the spray of his arterial blood bathing the right side of the bus. The blood loss was so quick, he was down and was unconscious within seconds. He was dead before Mike wiped the man's blood off of his Blackhawk Garra II knife, a folder with a nasty curved blade that he liked to keep razor sharp. So sharp, that the DHS agent never felt the slice that ended his life.

Mike retrieved the guard's handgun and opened the door. He leapt out into the fray, turning to his right. A large, bald shaved hoodlum was coming up the side of the bus at the same time. Both men were startled, but like most brawls, the bigger and stronger man usually won. In this case, Mike clobbered the punk on the bridge of his nose with the butt of his pistol. Blood spewed as Mike brought his left fist down on the man's face, breaking his cheekbone and crushing his eye socket.

All the years of listening to these racist's taunts was contained in that one blow. As a CO, he was trained to interact with the prisoners with respect. "Yes, prisoner Jones, you may do this" or "yes prisoner Smith that would be fine." Meanwhile, the bald white brothers would spit at him and call him nigger or yard ape. In general, Mike had to endure the constant and degrading abuse of a racist who had nothing to lose. The pent up anger from three years of listening to this nastiness was now unleashed.

Unexpectedly, Mike heard a grunt behind him. He quickly spun in time to find little Beth with the downed bus driver's baton. She had engaged another Aryan and was getting the best of the brute. In fact, she was damn good. A cross blow to his right knee had caused the grunt he had heard. Mike now watched approvingly as an uppercut to the thug's chin brought the piece of shit down. A coup de grace to the head split the man's skull depositing his brains on the concrete. She spun around to Mike and nodded.

"Got your back, brother. I was a CO too. Twenty years!"

Mike nodded back and the two entered the mass of people, trying to stop slaughter, Mike welding his pistol like a hammer and Beth bringing up the rear.

Suddenly, they heard a scream and turned to their left. Twenty yards away, they saw one of the Aryan brothers take a crowbar and smash it into the face of a young woman carrying a small girl. That was the last conscious thing Mike remembered until later when the carnage had been stopped. The red vision Mike first saw with the murder of the Captain and the judges flooded his brain. The criminals that DHS had unleashed on the unarmed people had crossed all the lines that civilized people use to define humanity. An unarmed mother was slaughtered for no reason. Mike went postal. It was the most incredible display of raw power Beth had ever seen. Men were tossed like rag dolls over the interstate and onto the road fifty feet below. Heads were smashed against anything hard enough to crack them. Car doors, concrete and even another head were used to terminate the criminals. He was a vengeful, giant god cutting a swathe through the chaff of humanity.

The brotherhood thug with the crowbar was just the first of over a dozen that felt his wrath. Mike picked up the crowbar that killed the young mother and ended the lives of the remaining Aryan brothers, allowing the remaining civilians to escape. Fortunately, the morass back at the original roadblock had kept those heavily armed agents occupied while Mike cleaned house to their rear.

Finally, when the bloodletting was through, Mike and Beth surveyed the damage. Six of the civilians had fallen, including the mother and her child, the later crushed by the mob as it tried to escape. Her little neck had been broken. All of the dozen or so Aryan Brothers lay dead somewhere nearby.

Mike finally dropped the crowbar and let Beth lead him back down the road, away from the roadblock.

"Come on, Mike." She gently said. "Let's get to OPD headquarters. There have to be some answers there."

Mike and Beth began the walk, followed by one person no one had seen. One other Aryan prisoner had escaped their notice. A freshly shaved man with a new tattoo on his arm and a swastika given to him by his new brothers. Under the swastika was a name: Beker. He was told it meant reborn, or converted in the German language, the language of the fatherland. Even though the real German word was Bekehrte, it was close enough. It meant more than conversion, it implied proselytization or active promotion of a faith or belief. The boy liked that. He now went by Beker.

CHAPTER 21

Day 6

Charlie

On the Road

As they approached the exit to John Young Parkway, the group could see the massive display of force that appeared to make the decision for them. There was no way they were going to be able to get by the military vehicles.

They cautiously approached the blockade and noticed a large group of people clogging the right side of the freeway. They weren't moving and Charlie could hear arguments between the people and the DHS soldiers.

"Come on," Charlie said to the others. "Keep right and let's find out what's going on over there. I like having options."

They agreed and pressed themselves to the right side of the thoroughfare, finally coming up to the barricade. A group of men were arguing with the agents, wanting to travel through to get home on the other side of the city.

"Sounds like a group we can join!" Janice said.

"I don't know," Theresa said. "I just want to get somewhere secure. I'm from Ohio. I don't need to get anywhere except where I can keep my children safe."

"We've discussed that," Janice replied. "You thought it would be smart to put some distance from the Disney refugees and your children. That there would be too many people with not enough food or supplies to handle everyone."

"I know, but seeing this makes me afraid. I mean, why can't we push through? Maybe they don't have any help further down. Otherwise, they would let us go through."

"I hate to say it, but Theresa makes sense!" Garrett said. "This makes me worried as well. I mean, what are they trying to do? Can't you hear it? Some of them are saying they live nearby and just want to go home."

The group was stuck. No one could come up with a clear reason for pushing forward and Theresa was getting more and more edgy.

"I'm sorry guys," Theresa finally said. "I have to get off. I'm taking my kids to the Fairgrounds. You guys need to do what you have to."

Janice gave me a resigned look and started to take little Brie off her shoulders when a commotion arose at the front of the group. The DHS agents began to part, moving several vehicles back and out of the way. It looked like they were going to let us through!

Before anyone could do a thing, the crowd behind us began to push forward. It felt like an ocean current grabbing us and pulling us out to sea. To fight it was hopeless and risked being trampled.

Theresa got a terrified look, but I yelled to her.

"Look," I said. "You can still get off at the next exit. The Fairgrounds will still be there if you want. Let's get out of this crowd and you can decide what to do."

She gave me a thumbs up and we let the crowd direct us through the opening and down the freeway.

A minute or two later, a scream ahead was our first warning that all was not right. Then several more people yelled that it was a trap. The next thing I knew, it felt like I was in a washing machine, my body being tossed about as people responded to the threat by racing more quickly down the road, turning to fight or even attempting to turn back to the DHS roadblock. I kept pushing forward along with Janice and Garrett. We hugged the far side of the roadway and tried to keep moving. Suddenly I heard a terrified cry and saw several bald men with clubs beating the people a few yards away. They were relentless and brutal. The crowd surged again and I lost sight of Theresa and Kaylee while barely keeping up with Janice, Garrett and Brie.

Out of the corner of my eye, I saw a giant of a man in a green uniform toss one of the tattooed men off the interstate. The criminal's screams were quickly cut short as he found the ground fifty or sixty feet below. I momentarily saw the giant man's eyes. They weren't human anymore as he went on a killing binge, smashing any of the bald tattooed thugs he laid his hands on. His actions gave us the opening we needed, and along with the others we quickly left the area and moved down the road.

I stopped the group after we had gone far enough to lose sight of the barricade so we could wait for Theresa to catch up with us. After 10 minutes, we became worried. After 15 minutes we were ready to go back for her when we saw two people moving down the roadway. Both were in uniform and I was about to yell for everyone to run, when I recognized the big man that was walking toward us. It was the giant that had killed all the thugs that were attacking us. They were moving at an unsteady gate, and the other officer, a small middle aged woman, was having some trouble helping her companion. Without thinking, I ran back to them and grabbed the man as he lumbered along between the disabled cars.

"Thanks dear!" The female officer said. Her green uniform had a corrections department patch and was stained with sweat and blood. The big man was huge. I wasn't sure I was helping all that much when Garrett came up and took over. The officer still towered over the kid, but Garrett was a bit over six feet tall and could give the large man a shoulder to use.

We quickly made it to Janice and Brie as they waited by a car.

"We have some water if you need it," I stated.

"That would be absolutely fabulous," the female said.

Both of them took a full liter of water, the big guy downing it in a few seconds and finishing off a second one in almost record time.

"Name's Mike Jones," he said, finally speaking for the first time since we met.

"Beth Hildreth," the female officer said. "And thanks for the water."

"Oh my God," Janice blurted out. "You saved our lives. Thank you!"

"And what was all that about?" She continued. "Why did they do that? I just don't understand!"

"We don't know either," Beth replied. "But you're welcome. Actually, you should thank Mike. I've never seen anyone wreak havoc like he just did."

"Dude," Garrett said, punching Mike on the shoulder. "You were a god out there! You were the Junk Yard Dog and John Cena all wrapped into one big killing machine! We would all be dead if it weren't for you."

"Hmmph," Mike replied.

He was still coming down from the fight and didn't have much to say right at that moment. Of course, as I would later learn, Mike has a tendency to not say much anyway. And "hmmph" tends to cover a lot of adjectives and emotions when he talks. Most of the time, though, he tends to act rather than speak. I respect that about the man.

"Hey!" Janice said. "Our friend is back there. Did you see her? She's about 30 years old, and has a little girl with her."

Beth gave us a very disturbed look and reached up and patted Mike on the back.

"No one's left alive back there," she solemnly said.

"NO!" Janice cried out, holding Brie in her arms. "Her mother is back there!"

"I'm sorry," Beth replied. "I really am. But there isn't anything we can do about that."

"Oh My God," Janice replied. "What am I going to do with her? Who's going to take care of this child?"

"Why don't you guys come with us to the Orlando Police Department? We'll get some help for the little one there. And maybe we can sort this all out."

"I don't like that plan at all!" Garrett said. "I just saw soldiers let a bunch of criminals lay into civilians and kill our friend. How can I trust the OPD?"

"I don't know kid," Beth continued. "But you can trust us." We aren't part of what's going on and I want some answers too! Just come with us. If things look hinkey, we can just keep going. But I'll tell you this; nothing is what it once was. Everything has changed and I want to know where we stand in all of this."

"I think we should do what Beth says," I said. "I know they are on our side and if everything is now different, I want to know how it's all changed so we can make a good decision about what to do."

After some more discussion, we all continued our journey and an hour later exited the freeway in downtown Orlando. We crossed back under I-4 and passed scores of military trucks parked under the freeway in the city owned parking lots that span the length of the elevated interstate.

"You guys stay here," Beth said as we got closer to the OPD headquarter building. "Mike and I will approach the building and get more information."

"Here," she continued and passed Mike a large envelope. "Your records. I got them from the bus."

"Thanks, Beth. I forgot."

"That's what a mother's for kid." She replied with a smile.

The two of them walked through the parking lot, across the street and up to the front door of the building where they were stopped by two DHS agents. After a minute, they were let in the building. Janice, Garrett and I hunkered down by a military vehicle, shaded by the interstate overpass above. Little Brie had fallen asleep on the walk, the two year old exhausted by the trip. She began to wake up and Janice took her to a secluded spot to potty. After they came back, we all used the spot to relieve ourselves and broke out our supplies to have some food and water.

Several hours went by and I was starting to get worried having heard nothing from either Mike of Beth.

"I think we need to keep moving," I said.

I had pulled out the map leading to our first bicycle trail. The bike path called Cady Way began a few miles from here and led us north for a considerable distance. I was mapping out a path through the city when Garrett tapped me on the shoulder and pointed to the front entrance. There, Mike and Beth were coming out, accompanied by one other man who wore the DHS military uniform. We had been ratted out! Beth and Mike had turned us in! Why else would they have a DHS goon with them?

Janice scooped up the little girl and we gathered our gear to escape back under the overpass and into the city skyscrapers behind us. Suddenly, a HUMVEE rolled in behind us from the other side of the expressway. We were trapped. If we moved away from Beth and Mike, the HUMVEE would see us. A gunner was operating the machinegun on top of the large jeep. They were idling right where we needed to go to escape into the city.

"What do we do?" Janice asked.

"I don't know," I replied.

"I know one thing," Garrett said. "I'm not getting taken without a fight."

He pulled out his Glock and checked the chamber for a live round.

"Put that away!" Janice hissed. "You start a gunfight and Brie could die! This is about more than you and me now!"

Garrett got an embarrassed look on his face and quietly put the handgun back in his belt.

"I guess we just wait and take our chances with DHS," I hesitantly said. "No other choice."

Mike and Beth rapidly approached with the unknown DHS agent.

"Hey guys," Beth quietly said. "I brought some help."

I stood up from behind the parked HUMVEE we were hiding behind and faced the three of them.

"Some help!" I stated. "You brought them right to us."

"I'm not one of them," the unknown man said. "I'm here to help."

"You sure don't dress the part of the white knight!" I shot back.

"White knight!" Mike said sarcastically. "You said I was a hero earlier, but I've never been called white before!"

His big stupid grin finally broke through my anger.

"Hey kid," the DHS guy said. "From what Beth and Mike told me, I understand. I'm surprised you didn't start shooting when I got into range."

"Garrett wanted to," I said as Garrett stood up as well. Then Janice rose from behind the military vehicle we had hidden behind holding Brie. "But Janice reminded me that we had to think of the kid."

"Hmmph," Mike said.

"Yeah," Beth agreed. "Smarter than they look, huh."

He approached and removed his battle helmet. He took off his tactical gloves and extended his right hand.

"My name is John Drosky," the DHS guy said. "A pleasure to meet you."

I took his hand and finally looked at his face. Wow! Nice. Handsome didn't quite cover it for me. More like yummy and dark and swarthy and every other adjective I could think of.

I guess I held his hand a bit too long from the snickers I got from several of my companions. I let go and blushed a bit, earning a few more chuckles. I quickly looked away, but I could tell John was still staring at me. A girl just knows.

"Anyway," John continued. "I have the keys to a condominium complex nearby. The DHS is clearing the city and pushing everyone into relocation centers. From what I can tell, they are separating the 'undesirables' from the rest of the population. Beyond that, it's above my pay grade."

"Who's undesirable?" I asked.

"Right now, I'm trying to figure that out. I've only joined the DHS today. I guess I passed their test because they've put me on the front line. I'm in training starting tomorrow, so I'll know more in a few days. In the meantime, let's get you guys situated. The condominium has running water but no power. You'll be the only ones in the building and since it's been marked as clear, you shouldn't get any visitors, so you should be fine. Just stay out of sight and stay quiet. This key will get you in the front door. All the rooms and individual condos are open so pick one with minimal visibility and some sound insulation."

"We need clothing and food for the little one here," Janice said.

"I'll work with Beth and Mike on the food." John replied. "As far as clothing, check the condos. The residents were forced to leave a few days ago and only could take one carry-on suitcase. You should be OK."

"How do we get in touch with you?"

"Leave a chalk mark on this pole over here," he said and pointed to an overpass concrete pillar. "Just put a 'J' on it and I'll get to your place as soon as I can. Otherwise, let's meet at your condo front door every night at 8 p.m. In a few days, we should have enough information to decide our best course of action."

After a brief private discussion, Janice, Garrett and I seemed to be in agreement. The worse that could happen is that we get a good night's sleep and leave the next day for the bike trails.

"Sure," I said, breaking from our little group. "Let's do this."

"I'll go find out what that HUVEE wants," John said as if reading my mind.

John walked to the vehicle and spoke with the driver. After a few seconds, the HUMVEE sped down the aisle of the parking lot and turned into a space. Within a minute, the driver and his gunner had entered OPD headquarters.

"OK," John said when he returned. "Just needed directions. They arrived from an armory down south and were unsure which building was DHS Headquarters. I guess the OPD symbol put them off."

"Yeah," I said. "With what I saw today, I don't doubt that they feared for their lives."

"You don't know the half of it!" Beth chimed in. "We'll all talk later. In the meantime, Mike and I are scheduled to get assignments tomorrow. We passed the test too, I guess."

"See you tomorrow night," I said and both groups moved their separate ways. I knew the condominium complex John had given us the key to. I had a friend who had lived there a few years before. It was only a ten-minute walk from here.

"Think they'll be OK?" Beth asked John as they made their way back to the OPD building.

"I think so," John said. "I deal with people all the time and they seem to have their act together. I mean, they are taking care of the kid and they were smart enough not to open fire when they saw me."

"Yeah," Beth hesitantly said. "But I do worry!"

"That's what mother's do!" Mike shot back, smiling at Beth.

"Tru dat, big man!" She replied with a smile.

"At least no one knows where they are!" John said.

No one, it seemed other than one other person. His freshly shaved head was starting to sunburn and beginning to itch. But he never noticed, having become intrigued with the group of four walking into the city in front of him. The two girls especially caught his attention. Yes, the girls. Those girls and their green surgical scrubs.

The pale ghost moved quietly behind the three as they shared holding their fourth little passenger. Their day was almost over; a safe destination lay just ahead!

The city was deathly quiet as the final leg of their journey as the condominium complex finally came into view. *Just in time*, thought Janice. *I'm dead on my feet.*

Or so the saying goes.

AUTHORS' NOTES

BY WALT BROWNING

We hope you enjoyed the book. Collaboration with another author was a first for both of us. Writing in tandem presented some challenges, but the obstacles were quickly overcome and we are happy with the results.

Our goal was to both entertain and inform. Charlie, in contrast to Morgan, is a city girl with little or no prepping knowledge. Her journey will involve a lot of learning on the fly, which will educate the reader on the potentially dangerous situations you may face as an urban environment.

If the response to the novella is positive, we are looking forward to more stories of Charlie and her fellow refugees as they struggle to survive in a hostile big city. The tricks and tradecraft needed to live in close quarters with millions of desperate people present an entirely new dynamic to the Going Home series. One that we hope you all enjoy.

Finally, we have included a chapter from Walt's first book, "The Book of Frank: ISIS and the Archangel Platoon." The story of a young, retired Marine who is drawn back to Iraq. He joins a group of operators hired to rescue a group of children trapped in a town controlled by ISIS. The book is available on Nook and Kindle.

Again, from both of us, thank you and enjoy.

Visit Walt Browning's website here:
http://www.waltbrowning.com

And Angery American's website here:
http://www.angeryamerican.com

THE BOOK OF FRANK:
ISIS AND THE ARCHANGEL PLATOON

CHAPTER 1

Tall Kayf, Iraq
January 7, 2015
"Sara"
5pm local time/8am EST

Sister Sanaa sat in a chair, taking inventory of her meager belongings. She brought these few personal items when she was forced to suddenly flee her convent in Mosul, when terrorists began purging Christians in her neighborhood late last November. She brought a large group of children with her that had taken refuge in a small town called Tall Kayf, a town 20 kilometers to the north.

From early summer to that fateful November day, their convent in Mosul was taking in displaced children. The parents of these poor children that ranged in age from 3 to 14 years had been slaughtered by ISIS in the towns to the south between Mosul and Baghdad. Fleeing to Mosul to find refuge, the tidal wave of jihad followed on their heels. With no one to stop them, and in many cases, getting support from the Sunni Muslims in the areas they conquered, ISIS claimed hundreds of miles of territory with almost no resistance. Often, they only halted their advance to fully cleanse the conquered populations before moving on, trying to guarantee that there was no significant enemy behind their advancing line.

With a population of 600,000, Mosul is one of the largest cities in Iraq, of which about 20,000 are Chaldean Catholic. Sister Sanaa was living in a convent in Mosul; that is until several weeks ago.

When ISIS arrived early that summer, over 10,000 Christians quickly left the city. Having only hours of warning, they gathered together what they could and fled the coming jihadist storm. Throughout the remaining summer and fall, the nuns kept a low profile, trying to help the remaining Catholics in the city.

Things went well at first. When ISIS initially invaded the city, the population was largely unaffected. Most of the Islamist wrath was still being directed at the cities to the south, and with battles outside Mosul, against a Kurdish Peshmerga resistance.

But in November, ISIS soldiers began walking the streets looking for Christian homes. When found, the homes were marked with a large letter "N" on the walls by their front door. "N" for Nazarene. Jesus was from Nazareth. The Chaldean convent received one of these marks, painted in bright red for all to see.

It took the insurgents several weeks to mark all the homes in the city's neighborhoods. Then, the Islamic soldiers began purging the Christian homes. Soon, soldiers appeared on the convent's street, so Sister Sanaa gathered the orphans who had been taken in by the order and brought them with her to Tall Kayf.

That town, about twelve miles north of Mosul, had a printing shop at the local Chaldean Catholic church. A weekly newspaper and fliers were produced there by the nuns, which helped connect the Chaldean community. Earlier that day, the other two nuns from her convent, Sister Nami and Sister Elishiva had been driven by a local volunteer to this church to use the printing presses. So when the terrorist soldiers appeared in her neighborhood, and with no motorized transportation available, Sister Sanaa and the orphans walked the eleven miles to find another safe haven. They joined the other two nuns in Tall Kayf.

~ * * * ~

A fortunate and wise move it was. Within two hours of leaving, Muslim soldiers raided the convent in Mosul they had just abandoned and blew it to rubble, taking with it millennia of irreplaceable history. This historic building the soldiers destroyed had been home to the nuns for over a hundred years, and was itself over a thousand years old. Made of stones from the local quarries, there was little to burn. Explosives, along with heavy military vehicles, leveled the convent. When they were finished, nothing was left. There would be no reminder of the blasphemous past for these Sunni conquerors. All traces of any of the kuffar, the unbelievers, was obliterated. Centuries-old manuscripts and artifacts were lost forever.

During the conquest of Mosul, the devastation of the non-believers was utter and merciless. Men were summarily executed; and women, depending on their age, were sold into slavery, raped and then killed or just shot on sight.

The children were subject to a slightly different fate. The rule was that if a child could talk, the child could convert. Those that chose to hold to their faith had their heads cut off. Little boys and girls, as young as two years old, were beheaded. Their bodies, still wearing their colorful dresses and preschool outfits, were left headless in the cross streets. Tiny victims of the Muslim jihadists.

For the older girls, the rules were different. If the girl was close to nine years old, she could be sold into marriage. Mohammed's reportedly favorite wife, Aisha, was six years old at the time of his marriage to her. He graciously waited until her 9th birthday before "consummating" the marriage. Mohammed was in his 50's at the time. Thus, 9 years old seemed like a good cut-off point for the conquering hoard.

The volunteer who drove the two nuns to Tall Kayf never returned. And with the arrival of Sister Sanaa with 14 orphans and no car, bus or truck, the nuns had no choice but to stay with the children and protect them as best they could.

A few days after they took refuge in Tall Kayf, ISIS forces arrived. An advance guard of over 70 terrorists came up from Mosul and frightened away or executed most of the Christian population, leaving a number of abandoned homes. One of these provided shelter to the 17 refugees while the church was sacked and the town cleansed of any further non-believers.

Tall Kayf, meaning "stone hill" in Arabic, had alley-way homes built into the side of the hill. These stone and white plaster buildings had been present for centuries, their foundations shaken over the years by earthquakes and attacked by floods. They lean, crumble and give the general impression that they could fall at any time; but they continue to stand, looking the worse for the wear.

One of these hillside homes belonged to a local Chaldean merchant, and was left empty when the family fled the city. A storage room sat in the back of the house, carved out of the side of the stone hill. The door to the room was hidden by wooden shelving. The nuns cleared the area leading to the storage room of anything of value and stacked worthless towels, trash and bottles on the shelves to help hide the doorway. After all were in the room, they pulled the shelving up against the wall from within the room and closed the door.

Sitting in the pitch-dark room, they could hear the invaders outside breaking and looting. Praying silently, the group held their place for the rest of the day and throughout the night. After dawn, when the last sounds of the raiders had not been heard in over 12 hours, they gently opened the door inward and slid the shelving unit away, allowing Sister Sanaa to search the house. Once the safety of the house was confirmed, they settled down to wait out the invaders and look for their chance to escape.

Six weeks later it was early January, and they were running short of food. Fortunately, the Islamic militia was relaxing its guard, having searched and secured the city. As the weeks passed, so did the invaders' interest with the town's occupants. The Islamists were more concerned with a growing threat from the Peshmerga militia that had taken back a town about eight miles to the north. That town, Bakufa, represented salvation to the nuns and the children in their care.

After pushing the Islamists out of Bakufa, a Christian militia was left to defend it. Called Dwekh Nawasha, which means, "We are the Sacrificers", they were the beginnings of an organized resistance. Tall Kayf thus was at the new front line of the war. Eight miles of no man's land stood between Sister Sanaa and freedom for her and the orphans that she was protecting.

With her food supplies desperately low, Sister Sanaa and the other nuns were forced to make a difficult decision. The nuns knew they needed to get to Bakufa, but who would risk the journey to get help?

"I don't think we can wait any longer," said Sister Sanaa. "We only have enough supplies to last a few more days. The abandoned homes are empty of food. We cannot risk another trip out of town for more. We have to get help."

"But who?" Sister Nami replied. "At my age, I could never make that trip on foot; and Elishiva would never hold up to the pressure. It is taking an act of God to keep her from falling apart as it is."

Sister Nami, well into her 70's, has taken the roll of "Mother Superior" or head of the convent. The walk to Tall Kayf from Mosul would have killed her. Even the walk to Bakufa, although several miles shorter, was out of the question. Sister Elishiva, who was in the other room with the children, was young enough to attempt it. But the nun had seen too much death already and her ability to cope with the possibility of discovery, rape and a painful death was too great to handle. Sister Sanaa, although slightly older than Elishiva, would be the only choice.

The problem was that an eight-mile journey would take her more than a day, both increasing the chances of discovery, and exposing her to harsh winter conditions. Further complicating things, Sister Sanaa had strained her aging hip on their original journey from Mosul. It was now completely inflamed and walking found her with a pronounced limp. Another long journey could well be her last.

Last night, it was well below freezing. Tall Kayf and the rest of northern Iraq can stay below freezing for many days in the winter. More importantly, with ISIS patrols scouring the northern half of the city, speed as well as silence were required. With Sister Nami too old, and Sister Elishiva too unstable, the journey would fall again onto Sister Sanaa. She was their only option.

"I will go," Sister Sanaa finally said. They all knew it was a death sentence, but they saw no other choice.

"Sister Sanaa, I can help" came a quiet voice. The two nuns turned to see one of the orphans standing in the doorway. Sister Sanaa stood up from her chair where she had been rummaging through her sack, looking for clothing for the expected journey.

Sara was the oldest of the orphans, having led three other parentless children north to Mosul from Bayji, a 114-mile journey. At 14, she was tall for her age, taller than any of the nuns, with dark brown hair and even darker eyes. They were eyes that had seen too much in her short time on this earth. She stood in the doorway, holding a coat and small sack folded over her arms.

Not yet a woman, and past being a child, Sara escaped from Bayji in June when ISIS overwhelmed the town. The terrorists attacked the town's government buildings, killing most of the people working there, including her mother. She never found out what happened to her father, other than being told by another refugee on the road to Mosul that he perished trying to get to her mother. No other details, just the information that he had been killed. She liked to think that he died valiantly, and that he was able to extract some revenge on the attackers. But this was probably only wishful thinking. Her father had not been a warrior. He had never held or fired a weapon as long as she could remember. He had been a merchant, owning a store that specialized in western imports.

His job had brought him into contact with many foreign individuals, including the American soldiers that had been in their town years before. With the expectation that the Americans would be with them for a while, he had even taught her English, at least enough to converse on a basic level.

When the Americans began to pull out of the area, it was a shock to him. No conqueror had voluntarily left Iraq that he could remember. History didn't work that way. First Nebuchadnezzar, the Babylonian king in the twelfth century BC to Alexander the Great in 331 BC, followed by the Muslims in the 7th century and the Ottoman Persians in the 16th century, Iraq was a land of the conquered. It only changed hands when it was conquered again.

When America abandoned the country, it didn't make sense to her father. It eventually led to his death when the American withdrawal left a power vacuum in the area. Like any vacuum, it was quickly filled. Unfortunately, it was filled by evil, nothing more than the pure, unadulterated evil called ISIS.

"No my child," says Sister Nami. "This is not your journey. We can handle this. Go back to the others and we will be out shortly. And tell Sister Elishiva that we want to speak with her."

"But Sister Nami, I have done this before. I can do it again." she replied. There was no pleading or fear in her voice, just a simple statement of fact. "I can be there in less than a day. I promise I can do it," she states.

"No Sara, I cannot take that chance" Sister Nami replies bluntly.

"Sister Nami, I can travel more quickly than anyone here. I know this town and how to escape it. I have been with you to find food. You know I am quiet and can avoid being caught. Please let me do this. You have done so much for us. It is time I did something for you and the others" she flatly explains.

"Sister Nami" Sister Sanaa whispers. "We should talk about this."

"Absolutely not!" Sister Nami whispers forcefully back. "This is not up for discussion."

"Sister Nami and I must discuss this Sara. Go tell Sister Elishiva to come in here so we can tell her the plan we're considering," Sister Sanaa tells the young orphan. Sara returned to the hidden room where the orphans and Sister Elishiva were staying.

After Sara disappeared, Sister Nami was about to say something when she was cut off by Sister Sanaa.

"Sister Nami," she says quickly. "She is right. She has the best chance to save the other children. This is not about us and our lives. It is about the orphans."

"We can NOT put her in that kind of danger," Sister Nami says.

"We must do what has the best chance of survival for these children!" Sanaa replies. "On our journey up here from Mosul, I had difficulty keeping up with the children. That trip damaged me. Now, I don't know if I can even make it to Bakufa. Perhaps, if I could rest on the way, or if there were not a time constraint, I could do it. But with the need for stealth, I doubt I can make it past the patrols."

"And," she continued, "we do not have the luxury to hope I can get past the guards blocking the northern end of town and then make the 8-mile walk. Our food is nearly gone; or at least there is not enough to prevent these children from starving in the next week or two. And who knows how long it will take for help to arrive."

The elder nun didn't like where this was going. The anger she felt at the situation was almost unbearable. She wasn't blaming God, but couldn't understand why this was happening. This horror she was living in. This nightmare was a test of her will and patience, and she was about to run out of both.

"I just can't imagine sending Sara," Sister Nami stated. "It goes against every belief I have. Everything I am tells me not to send her."

"If you believe in saving these children," Sister Sanaa replied, "then you must ... WE must do what has the best chance for success."

Both nuns went silent and contemplated their situation. On a logical level, Sister Nami knew that sending Sara was their best chance of rescue. She couldn't get past the desire to protect them all. She, and she alone was responsible for their safety.

Just then, Sister Elishiva came in with a questioning look on her face.

"Sara sent me in, what is it?" she asks.

"We are at the end of our food," Sister Sanaa states. "It is too dangerous to venture out again and forage for more. Last week we were almost caught, and all the abandoned homes around us have been searched."

"In fact," the nun continued, "I am worried that we may have been seen by one of the town people. I don't know if they knew who we were; but when we passed by the church, there was someone in the cemetery that looked our way as we passed up the street. If they told the terrorists, there will be no stopping them from finding us in the next few days."

"That would explain why we saw the men patrolling this area of town yesterday. I wondered why they were here," Elishiva said. "I hadn't seen them for over a week."

"Then time is critical," Sanaa said. "Someone has to go now."

"I will go," Sister Elishiva suddenly says. "I am the youngest, and I have the best chance to get there."

After she finished, she put a thin smile on her face and turned abruptly to leave the room.

"Just a moment, Sister," Sister Nami said. "Please stay so we can talk."

Sister Elishiva stood silently, facing away from the other two nuns. She slowly started to turn back towards them. Within seconds, the poor nun started to gently shake. She tried to look at her two friends, but could only keep her eyes cast down on the floor in front of them. She tried to speak, to reassure them that she would be alright, but the words didn't come. They were stuck in her throat like some vise was tightening around her chest, keeping her breath from coming out. She finally looked up, and the terror and panic of the situation showed starkly on her face. She was in the early stages of a panic attack, and was praying and fighting to keep it at bay. It wasn't working.

"Sister Elishiva, my dear and sweet Elishiva...." was all that Sister Nami could say. She went forward and embraced the trembling nun, whispering into her ear and soothing her.

"This is not your battle, my friend," she said. "This is not your cross to bear. We need you here with the little ones. They need you. They trust you more that the two of us!"

Sister Elishiva looked up into Nami's eyes, questioning and afraid.

"Then who is to go? Who is to bring us help? Who is going to save us," she blurted. They were both silent for a moment or two, then Sister Nami looked at her and smiled.

"Sara," Nami replied. "Sara will save us."